ABOUT TH

'Bernard Ashley's greatest gift is to turn what see......
low-key realism into something much stronger and more
resonant.' Philip Pullman on *Tiger Without Teeth* in
the *Guardian* Book of the Week feature

Bernard Ashley is one of the most highly regarded
authors in this country. Born in Woolwich, south
London, he was evacuated during the war, and ended up
attending fourteen different primary schools. After
school, Bernard did National Service in the RAF where
he 'flew' a typewriter. He then went on to become a
teacher and later a headteacher – his two most recent
posts being in east and south London, areas which have
provided him with the settings for many of his books.
Bernard now writes full time.

Bernard Ashley's other novels for the Black Apple list
include *Little Soldier*, shortlisted for the *Guardian*
Children's Book Award and the Carnegie Medal, *Revenge
House* and most recently *Freedom Flight*.

ALSO BY BERNARD ASHLEY

FREEDOM FLIGHT

LITTLE SOLDIER
*Shortlisted for the Carnegie Medal and
the Guardian Children's Book Award*

REVENGE HOUSE

ORCHARD BOOKS
96 Leonard Street, London EC2A 4XD
Orchard Books Australia
32/45-51 Huntley Street, Alexandria, NSW 2015
ISBN 1 86039 563 5 (hardback)
ISBN 1 84362 204 1 (paperback)
First published in Great Britain in 1998
First paperback publication in 1998
This edition published in 2003
Text © Bernard Ashley 1998
The right of Bernard Ashley to be identified as the author
of this work have been asserted by him in accordance with the
Copyright, Designs and Patents Act, 1988.
A CIP catalogue record for this book is available from the British Library.
1 3 5 7 9 10 8 6 4 2 (paperback)
Printed in Great Britain

TIGER
WITHOUT TEETH

BERNARD ASHLEY

ORCHARD BOOKS

I should like to thank Ed Wingrave the cycling pro for all his help with technical details – and for letting me call my fictitious bike a *Wingrave*.

Chapter One

"**B**OOVE!"

"What?"

"You know what!"

"I don't, do I?" But Davey Booth did. He might as well have had 'hand-built Wingrave' tattooed across his forehead.

"Bell tells me you've nicked my wheels." Stuart Jarvis – Hard Stew – even smelt violent.

"I 'aven't!"

"You makin' Bell a liar?"

"I've got *my* wheels ..."

"*My wheels!* I 'ad my name on that bike."

"Well, that's down to Bell ..."

"Shut it! It's down to you, an' your poxy ol' man waving 'is dosh at Bell's ol' lady – that's who ..."

And Davey made the mistake of shrugging, starting to walk away; his stomach going round like candyfloss in a drum. Stuart Jarvis punched him in the mouth with a fist like a knuckleduster. Blood, spit, split lip, all the works – and Davey standing staring into Jarvis's cold eyes.

"I want that Wingrave, son – an' that little smack's for starters." And Jarvis sauntered off, not a toss given for any school punishment which might come his way. What difference was a few days' suspension to him, even if the head *did* dare to face his old lady?

It was all about Carl Bell's Wingrave, the one with the hand-built frame. Carl was moving up to oval tubing, so he'd put a free advert in *Cycling Plus* and he was asking three hundred for what he'd got, just as Davey Booth was starting on the serious track. Up to now Davey had been borrowing the club fixed wheels over at Herne Hill velodrome, and he'd really got the taste for that old freeze on the front teeth they called racing – now the time was right for getting something sleeker of his own for road and circuit stuff: and didn't Carl Bell's Wingrave look ready-made with its spare racing wheels? *And* it was the right price for Christmas and birthday combined, if he could get fifty for his mountain bike. Sweet!

The sour was, Hard Stew was on the same trail. He'd seriously buckled his bike in a row with a Transit van and twisted his front forks like dreadlocks. But because of what his mother was like, the Transit driver had paid up sharp, and Hard Stew was standing there with cash in hand. The result being, Davey and Hard Stew were both in for Carl Bell's bike, and both were waving the asking price. Except that Davey didn't know who the other buyer was.

This was when Davey's father had moved things on, the way he always had to. He'd taken Davey round to Carl's house, seen the bike and given it the nod; and to stop Carl's mother havering about, he'd gone to three twenty-five to knock anyone else out of the frame. He'd moved things on all right – and moved Davey's life down the road to hell.

Because if Davey had known it was Hard Stew also in with the asking price, he'd have come straight off the sprinters' line and let him through. People did give way to Hard Stew. But all Carl Bell had said, until Davey was wheeling the Wingrave out of the front door, was he'd got someone else wanting it – no other name given, up to then.

"Hard Stew? You joking?"

Because Hard Stew was no reference to school meals. Stuart Jarvis was called Hard Stew on account of how he hit you. He was as hard as paving slabs, a Year Seven Rottweiler among the spaniels – scaring the kids, scaring the teachers, scaring the head. The only person he didn't scare was his mother, because that's where it all came from.

"*Stuart Jarvis?* Why didn't you say?"

"You never asked."

But once Davey's dad had moved things on, there wasn't any going back.

So Davey had waited like a man on death row for Hard Stew to find out. Which hadn't taken long.

Davey's grandad would have known what to do – and done it. Without involving the school, he'd have gone round and sorted Hard Stew himself, old as he was – Mrs Jarvis or no Mrs Jarvis.

But by then the old man was sedated out of his pain with morphine, a day off death, and when he'd looked at Davey he'd been content with the official word on the split lip.

"Rugby. Got in the way of a boot."

Or *had* he swallowed it? Hadn't Davey thought the old man's hand on the blanket had bunched itself up into a fist?

Davey couldn't help himself – he jumped when the electric curtains started to draw across. He'd been holding his breath, waiting for the preacher to go for the button, but when the curtains jerked he still jumped – and went so light in the head he thought he might go over.

But he held on and stared his eyes dry so as not to lose any sight of the coffin, not till the last crack of curtain had closed. He wanted to say "See you, Grandad" under his breath, but he couldn't, not with all the tears and nose and the lumped-up throat. It would have come out like a shout.

When the hearse had come to the door with Grandad in it, Davey had been racked with a pain like nothing he'd ever known. Seeing that polished coffin with Davey's own bunch of cornflowers up there on the lid – that had been the lowest point of his life; till those curtains had just closed on the man.

Davey pictured his grandad lying in there, his eyes shut like for a Sunday nap, the bald head with the short trim, the big nose he stroked when he was about to knock you back in a board game, the mouth that must have got twisted the way it had from all that smiling out of the side.

Gone.

For ever.

Like a lot of kids, Davey had had two grandads. There'd been this one, Grandad Sam, and there was his dad's dad, Grandad Ilford – named after where he lived, because he didn't like the sound of Wally. But they didn't see so much of him, coming from the other side of the river; only when they had to.

And there was never any confusion over the Nans – Grandad Sam's wife had died before Davey was born, a mystery no one ever talked about, and he only knew her face from photographs, that pretty young woman who was always going to be younger than his mum was now.

Davey looked at his mum along the row of black. He'd been so screwed up himself that he hadn't paid her a lot of attention; but she seemed to be all right – she hadn't broken down, was standing there with her blonde hair piled up in a black silk ribbon – and she'd managed to sing 'Abide With Me' and say all the amens; which was more than Davey had. Davey could no more have trusted his voice than he'd have trusted Stuart Jarvis not to hit him again.

Because they'd been a special pair, Davey and his grandad; "the chaps", as the old man had called them. Partners. Oppos. Davey had spent more time round at the old people's bungalows than anyone else in the family. His grandad had changed his settee for a sofabed for all the nights Davey stayed; and like a regular in a pub, Davey had his own little tankard in the kitchen, as well as the freedom of the fridge.

"Amen," everyone said, and thin organ music started to come out of the air conditioning. The tall man with the top hat and gloves had walked to the front and was inviting Davey's mother to lead the way out and shake hands with the preacher.

"Come on. Leave that." From his dad.

Davey put down the Order of Service, and after a quick tidy with a tissue, did a sideways step in line behind his mum.

"They make a lovely show." This was Auntie Rene at the wreaths and sheaths, which were all laid out round a small post with Davey's grandad's name on it. *Samuel George Butler.* She was stooping to find her own tribute, with quick looks to see who'd gone dearer.

Davey knew his cornflowers wouldn't be there – they'd ridden into the furnace with Grandad, the same colour as his eyes.

He walked on, away from it, went to stand by the funeral car which would take them back home. He wanted away now, because going by the smoke coming out of the chimney, Grandad wouldn't be Grandad any more.

An old girl from the bungalows came over and gave Davey a bristly kiss.

"You was very special to him," she said; but she went away when Davey didn't talk back, or cry.

He looked over the boxed fir hedge, over the top of Shooters Hill, back in the direction of the route they'd taken in the cars, where they'd passed the bungalows with its line of neighbours standing to see the old man off.

Davey had hardly been able to look. The bungalows were built in a gap in the houses where there had once been a church. And with a choke in his throat Davey remembered how, if he'd ever said something out of order, his grandad would say, "Watch your back, son, this is holy ground." But when the old man was drinking his stout, he'd whisper, "Holy water!" to the lifted glass.

It was always different, round at Grandad's, different to being at home. Davey had more rope, was treated more grown-up. On Saturdays when there wasn't a cycling club run "the chaps" always had a look at which horses were in the frame; and when Davey slept over he got to see films they never let him see at home. On the eating front, Grandad sizzled bacon and soaked slices of white bread in the fat, devil's diet in Davey's house. "Get in the food-boat!" his grandad would say. And Davey had loved all those other old sayings: he didn't *make a sandwich*, he *knocked up a sarny*; he didn't *answer* the door, he *saw to it*; he went to the *khazi*, not the lav; and he never read a *book*, he had a *reader* on the go. But if Davey ever said any of them at home, he'd get a hard out-of-order look from his dad.

Also, his grandad didn't dress like the other old boys. He wore the sort of clothes old men in Spain wore; *young* old men, active; silky shirts, and what he called his "slacks". And trainers; he wore trainers as if he was always ready to have it away on his toes.

Davey looked back at the cluster of people talking over the flowers. A bit of smiling was going on; none of those people were exactly broken up by Sam Butler going. Even Davey's mum was well in control. *Well* in control.

She was talking to Uncle Cyril. *Great* Uncle Cyril who ran a pub – a tall man with a big Adam's apple which he'd scratched shaving, and wearing the same sort of funeral coat the under-takers wore. He was filling his pipe, ready for the off; knocked out his dottle on the cremation before last. Davey had seen him for the first time in ages today; *and* up close, because the man was put in the same car as Davey, the second limo, riding with cousin Claire: whose other grandad was

Davey's. Not that Davey had ever seen much of her, either.

The four of them had come all the way without anyone saying a word – Davey too upset; Claire looking out of the window; Uncle Cyril staring ahead with his mouth shut tight like a man who'd zipped it.

She was pretty, Claire, in a slinky grey coat and a black bow on her tight-back ponytail, looked every bit the funeral party: made Davey feel elbowed, because she wasn't anywhere *near* equal to him in knowing Grandad.

"He was *my* grandad, and I loved him," he wanted to shout at everyone. "We were 'the chaps', him and me! Sam Butler and Davey Booth…"

But he didn't. He stood scuffing his shoes while the group round the tributes gradually got eased towards the cars.

The man in the top hat ushered Davey's parents and two aunts into the first limo. And, copying his dad, Davey let Top Hat usher Claire into their car first, then Uncle Cyril next, before he went to get in himself: which had Claire sliding across the seat to make room. And no doubt she couldn't help it, but her slinky coat got caught under her bottom, and Davey saw what he wasn't meant to; a quick flash of black knickers.

Class! Grandad would've winked at that. And Davey hoped like hell he hadn't said "Ooer!" like he thought he had; and he was only just getting over it, cursing in his head for being the sort of kid who went beetroot at anyone saying "bra", when Uncle Cyril suddenly turned his world upside down.

He rapped the stem of his pipe on the window and looked back at the crematorium.

"Well, let's hope the old devil rots in blazes!"

The red drained from Davey's face; his stomach came up to throttle his throat. White with anger, he stared at the man. *What the hell do you mean by that?* he wanted to yell at the old goat. Bad mouthing your own family? *Wishing Grandad for ever in hell fire?* But Uncle Cyril was back to rattling his pipe on his teeth, with the sort of face on which stopped anyone talking to him.

Chapter Two

HELL FIRE or not, Hard Stew wasn't going to go away. The threat of him sat on Davey's head like some heavy helmet he had to wear; because what Hard Stew wanted, Hard Stew got. Any grieving Davey might have done by riding it out on his new bike had the brakes slammed on by the thought of Hard Stew Jarvis waiting round the next corner. He didn't live far, and these streets were Jarvis's streets. Already, Davey's Wingrave was like a new Sega without the batteries.

Which left Davey moping round the house, missing his grandad and brooding over and over on those words, *let's hope the old devil rots in blazes.* Until his dad told him to "Snap out of it, for God's sake!" But the last thing anyone can do is snap out of grief. Grief can only be *smoothed away*, worn off, it's never snapped out of.

And the skies would fall before Hard Stew was ever smoothed away.

"You done what I said?" Jarvis bad-breathed on the Monday, pulling Davey in the corridor – and just see Dan Brewer, Davey's mate, slink off quick to the next lesson!

"Done what?" Davey kept his distance, was going to make Hard Stew come at him.

"You givin' me the two fingers, Boove? Told your ol' man you got the 'ump wi' Bell's bike?"

"Not as yet."

"Well, don' dwell, son, don' dwell, 'cos I'm getting a pain wi' you ..." And Hard Stew got him, anyway, with a kick on the kneecap.

"Ow!"

"'Ow!' 'e says. *Ow*'s only gonna be the start of it!"

And from the look in Jarvis's eye, looking round to his creepy crawlies who'd hung about, his Loyals, Davey reckoned this wasn't even about the bike any more. It was about *power*, it was about people doing what Jarvis wanted: about what crooks like him called respect, and control.

Davey watched the kid go spitting his way along the corridor to extra English. He rubbed his knee, which didn't hurt half as much as he'd put on. But seeing that swaggering back, he saw the hopeless fix he was in. Because while he *could* tell his dad about the aggravation, he knew his dad would only look down on him from a great height and tell him not to be scared of some *kid*.

Stuart Jarvis and whose army? He's only another boy isn't he? Just because Hard Stew was only a kid to Davey's dad, the man couldn't see how much harder he was to Davey.

Which was a facer for Davey that evening.

His mum and dad were getting their jackets on to go round to the bungalow for the family clear-out, when who squealed his brakes outside the house but Dan Brewer – skin shorts, Centurion lid.

"Coming out for a spin round the common?"

The last place Davey *wanted* to be was in that bungalow without his grandad there; and definitely not seeing the emptying of the drawers. The last place! But only the last place except round the streets, out and about on the hand-built Wingrave. Because, wouldn't Brewer do a sprint when Jarvis suddenly showed? And Hard Stew *would* show. He patrolled the streets nights the way he'd got the school yard covered days. Ever since the Wingrave had been brought back to Davey's, Jarvis had been out and about at all hours, cruising his old Dawes like a hit man on the wait.

But Davey wasn't up to facing that truth, even to himself. He really believed the answer Brewer got.

"Sorry, mate, tucked up. Going round my grandad's, sorting out his bits." Telling himself that Uncle Cyril was going to be there, and if he used his ears he might get some clue to why the man had bad-mouthed his grandad.

Which was the state Davey was in. He was desperate to know what the old goat had meant, but it took the frights of Hard Stew to get him on to it.

They'd left the curtains up, but the bungalow still had that *gone away* look. Gone away for ever.

It was a warm evening, the middle of May. Davey's mother let them in with her key and bustled through to show how she wasn't planning to get upset. Davey's father went direct to reading the meters in the kitchen cupboard. While Davey stood in the hallway and took in Grandad's smell. *Old Holborn*; his favourite roll-up, his 'snout' – which had killed him, no doubt. But the smell *was* Grandad; and to Davey it was as if he could talk to it. *Wotcha, mate!*

A car tooted outside; which would be Auntie Glad – and when it went on tooting, Davey put his head round the front door.

"Give us a yard. Tell your dad to give us a yard." Uncle Cyril was shouting; they wanted room to park without blocking the residents' road to their sheds. And not only Uncle Cyril in the car, but Cousin Claire sitting in the back.

What was this sudden taste in Davey's mouth – like medicine with iron in it?

Davey shouted the message and watched the girl getting out, not showing her knickers this time. She gave a little wave to Davey as if they'd known each other all their lives. Which they had, except only as cousins who'd hardly ever met: Davey had definitely never *noticed* her before, till the day of the funeral.

Uncle Cyril fiddled about in his glove compartment and Auntie Glad was at the boot with a couple of empty suitcases, while Claire came in through the gate and up to Davey at the front door.

Davey swallowed the new taste.

"Hiya!" he said.

She wasn't in black today. Far from it. She was in a sharp orange majorette skirt, a white T-shirt, and a waistcoat. The sort that doesn't do up.

She came up to him, and for one blood-thumping moment he thought she was going to give him a cousinly kiss.

"*Sad*, isn't it?" she said, a quick face to go with it.

"You can say that again."

And he could see she was tempted to do just that, for the laugh. She had that sort of buzz about her.

They went through into the kitchen; in came Uncle Cyril and Auntie Glad; and the kettle was put on.

Davey looked at his mum, and his dad. Ever since Grandad had died; no, since before then, since his illness had taken him to his bed and then to the hospital, they'd never lost their *busy-busy-busy* look. Too busy to talk to one another; too busy to talk to Davey; too busy to give anyone long on the phone.

That had to be what your dad dying was like – the way Davey's mum was taking it, the same as she'd pulled the shutters down on Nan dying young. But it meant there was no way he could ask *her* what Uncle Cyril had meant in the funeral car. Nor his dad: if his dad had heard, it would have started a riot. Which was why Davey would have to keep his ears open instead.

But, here was Claire – she'd gone home from the funeral with Uncle Cyril and her mum – so might the man have opened up a bit more after, to her?

And Davey said it before he'd given himself

time to think: because he'd never have had the neck to say it if he'd planned it.

"Want to come out the back?"

Claire didn't bat an eyelid. "*If* you like."

"Just – out the way."

"I *know* what you mean." She gave Davey's dad a beaut of a smile while Davey found the back door key on its secret nail in the crockery cupboard. At night, he'd been the one to check that the door was locked while the chaps watched the television in the front. *"Don't want no hobbit taking liberties!"*

The garden was small, and well looked after. Somewhere, Grandad had learned how to grow things. It was neat, like a little park, bright with geraniums and roses. "My yard of sky," he'd say to Davey, sitting in an old-fashioned deck chair and closing his eyes up to the sun. "Sweet, Davey boy – a yard of sky to look at."

Except to Davey the sky was just the sky, always up there somewhere. A good smooth track was more his line in heavens, where aero-rims whined and you could hit the blue sprinters' line somewhere near the front.

"Small, but *very* nice." Claire was referring to the garden.

"He liked it out here."

"Pooh! What *is* that?"

The shed still smelt of wood stain. The chaps stained it every year, Grandad high, Davey low, no drips thank you. It was one of the last things they'd done together.

"What's *in* there?"

"The usual."

"Home-brewed beer and manly magazines? That's what's in ours." Claire tried to see through the net at the window. "Calls it his hell hole, my *dear* dad."

Which Davey suddenly jumped at. Sent from above! He fumbled for the plastic-wrapped key in its hiding place in the rockery. "Talking about hell holes ..."

"Why, are you a bit of a devil?" Claire gave him the big eyes. "'Cos I'm not coming *in* there if you are!"

"No!" Red face again – red as a Coke can. "It's just, what Uncle Cyril said. In the funeral car."

"Did he say *anything*?"

Davey turned the key. "He said, 'Let's hope he rots in blazes.'"

"*Did* he? I don't hear him, most of the time." Claire had gone into the shed. "*Nice* smell, you could say." She looked about. "Hello, what's this?"

23

"He was talking about Grandad." Davey followed her in.

"No, I don't hear half *he* goes on about." She was pulling an elderly Claud Butler off the shed side. "*Some* bike!"

And it was. Oiled, maintained, the tyres not far off the pressure.

"He used to go to the post office on it. And come out on runs with me."

"You *into* bikes?"

"Could say."

Claire had lifted the Claud Butler to the middle of the shed and was suddenly gripping Davey's shoulder as she straddled it.

"Got a hand-built Wingrave," Davey said, for something to take his mind off this touch.

"Which hand? *Who's* showing off, then?"

"It's a bike."

"What else? Not here, is it?"

"At home."

Claire bent to the half drops, fitted one trainer into a toe clip. "Well, *that's* not far. We'll go and get it and clear off for a ride."

That funny taste in Davey's mouth again. Claire, all leg and sweet smile, Davey in a new yard of heaven with his cousin ...!

But there was no way Davey could go out on

the road with Jarvis about; and definitely not with Claire along: if the thug saw the pair of them and gave chase, Davey couldn't go racing off on a hare and hounds. Saturday or Sunday mornings, OK, when Jarvis would still be in his pit; but not on a Monday evening when he'd be round the next corner. Davey had meant it when he'd seen off Dan Brewer.

"Oh, I dunno ..."

"You dunno *what*, Mr Hand Built? Give me a crossbar back to your place and get your bike. They're going to be *all* evening in there ..."

Which was true. And think of having Claire on your crossbar!

But none of that saw off the fact of Hard Stew.

"No, sorry – haven't got two lids."

"Please yourself – I'm *not* begging." All up in the air. Claire came off the bike – managed it without Davey's shoulder this time – and clattered it back against the shed wall. She stepped round Davey and swished back into the bungalow; leaving him to lock up the shed and put the key back among the alpines. Inside out at his cowardice.

"How many house keys did he have?" Auntie Glad was ignoring her mug of tea and pushing on.

"I can slip them in to the Council after the weekend."

"There's mine," Davey's mother said, "and his own. Did you have a set?"

Auntie Glad shook her head. "Never been local enough."

"Then it's just the two sets."

"Plus the shed key hidden *in* the rockery," Claire told them.

"Stashed away, more like," said Uncle Cyril, with that look he'd had on since he'd got there, like someone trying not to breathe in someone else's breath.

"Only being handy," Davey told them, "in case he went out without his others." It was part of his grandad's plan for emergencies. The shed key let him into the shed, where there was a front door key hidden behind a sawn-off bolt in an upright; the third bolt from the top on the left side of the door.

But, looking round at these sifters and clearers, Davey reckoned he wasn't going to let on about that.

"How, *handy?*" his Dad was asking.

"If it was raining, he could sit in his shed till Mum got in from work."

"Never happened once."

"No. Because he'd know *all* about keys," Uncle Cyril said.

"Anyway, we'll need it," Auntie Glad decided; and it was Claire who went out to get it.

Back of the pack, lapped, off the track – that was how Davey felt. Of all the people in the world, *he* was the one who should have been in and out of Grandad's cupboards and drawers, sorting his stuff. He should have been fetching any keys. *He* was the other half of "the chaps".

All the same, leaning there like a bent frame, he knew why he hadn't let on about the secret key to the front door. He'd just made up his mind. He was coming back on his own, before the house-clearance people came on Saturday, and he was going to walk round these rooms, just him and his grandad's ghost, and he was going to do what he couldn't do tonight – remember him properly. He'd take a chance on Jarvis, and he'd pay his private respects to the man he'd loved to bits.

Right now, though, he got out of their way and found the armchair in the living room, and a book – any old book, one on keeping budgies, which his grandad had never done – and he tried to close his ears to the sounds of drawers opening and closing on the other chap's things: his old penny whistle, the draughts and the poker dice, and the playing cards with the nudes on and the thick rubber band around; all the stuff that had once been special to the two of them.

And what wouldn't he give for the smell of a freshly lit snout ...?

Chapter Three

GEOGRAPHY WITH Spasm Spinoza, Tuesday afternoon, mapping, and Davey was feeling easy. He wasn't *enjoying* the lesson because these days he wasn't enjoying anything; but even in all the grief he was being given, there were times which weren't as dire as others; and this was starting to feel like one of them.

First, he'd got through a morning without Hard Stew bombing round a corner; and if pigs could fly, Davey would have been hoping he'd got someone else on his hit list. Jarvis was keeping his head down at the back of the room right now, no doubt on some scam of his own.

Second, the mapping they were doing was simplifying an Ordnance Survey sheet to show just the contours, drawing with special pens on cartridge paper – which was good for the soul, seeing that shiny black ink dry slowly – plus, you didn't need to have your brain in gear. A good eye, a steady hand, all that stuff – but it didn't amount to much more than copying, so the mind could roam.

Definitely a shaky contour at the start, with the quick thought as ever of Uncle Cyril; but now Davey's mind had started roaming over Claire. And a few more shakes; because, what a great chance he'd elbowed with that girl, what a prize hobbit he'd been! He couldn't have been thinking straight, blowing out a run on their bikes with a girl like Claire. Him and her, and a Coke in Gerry Gelato's. As it was, he'd stayed in his grandad's living room mooning over budgies until the sisters had finally driven off in their different directions. And not another look from Claire: nothing nose-in-the-air, but just *elsewhere* all the time.

He rested the heel of his hand on the blotting paper, and while his fingers copied the contours from the Landranger sheet, his mind ran through a tasty little scene, a definite daydream, the sort people worked on before they went to sleep – a little number where he got back in with Claire, where he wasn't so *sad*. A smart little story where she'd gone up this tree, after a cat which had got itself stuck. Her cat, something she loved. And there she was, with the cat in her jacket, sitting in a fork and suddenly not able to get back down; with no one else around, of course, because we

were talking *remote*, up on the edge of Oxleas
Wood ...

Meanwhile, take the 50-metre line through to
Birling Place, dipping, and then up to Paddles-
worth ...

*Into the story he came, on a cyclo-cross training
run, greeny brown eyes big and clear, dark hair
hanging handsome over his lean face. All that.*

"Excuse me!" from the princess in the tower.

Davey stopped and looked up.

"Look who's stuck!"

*"Hang about." Davey leaned his bike, climbed
the tree; but to get to the cat, which he'd have to
rescue first, he had to inch himself out along
another branch, big drop, life at risk.*

"Be careful!"

"Don't worry."

Now take the ink on through to Lad's Farm and
west of Upper Halling; dip the pen, keep the line
alive ...

*He took the cat, which knew him for a friend so
didn't struggle, put it in his cycling top, and climbed down with it. Now it was back up the tree to
help guide Claire's foot down to the branch below,
which she hadn't been able to reach – meaning he
had to hang one-handed like Tarzan, where losing
his grip would crash him down to his doom.*

And the line goes back on itself round the Quarries, which comes to a highish point. He'd been out here on runs with the club . . .

"Man! How's that for brave!"

Davey did a little bow. "Not really." And with a mixture of strength and sheer courage he helped Claire to safety at the foot of the tree.

"I'd have been all right without the cat," she said, smiling with those white teeth. "But so glad I wasn't."

"Glad? Why?"

"Because now I can kiss you to say thanks." Very matter-of-fact.

Another dip, keep it wet and gleaming . . .

And she put her arms round his neck and her lips came up to his, as natural as you like; and she closed her eyes, and—

The back of Jarvis's clenched hand scuffed itself across the cartridge to smear the wet black of Davey's work into a wiped arc. He clobbered on to the front of the class, sticking his blackened fist in his pocket, told Spasm Spinoza he was going to the lav, and went.

Spasm called OK – they all said OK to Jarvis. Davey swore and looked at his ruined map; at thirty minutes of wasted effort. And at the reminder that Jarvis hadn't gone away.

Neither had Spasm, who was doing a quick circuit before the bell.

"Oh, dear, Mr Booth. What's happened here?"

Davey looked up at him; at the designer glasses and the draped scarf.

"My stupid elbow!" he said; sick that he didn't even *think* about telling the truth.

"Have you got inks at home?"

"Yeah."

"Then take another piece of paper – which isn't cheap. And I'll see it tomorrow – tell your elbow."

And that was how stupid male chauvinist daydreams ended up. All shame and frustration.

Tuesday nights were John Booth's cricket nights. After he'd driven off in his whites, Davey could relax from watching every word he said and take up a bit more space. There was always a different feel in the house when his dad was out. Apart from the Reach Wheelers club night on a Thursday, Tuesday was one of the nights when he hadn't used to go round to his grandad's.

Tonight Davey had shown the true Booth spirit of moving things on; he'd got out his homework while his dad changed, the map first, and he'd sat looking busy as he shouted cheerio. But as soon as the revving died, he rested his pen and put his mind to Hard Stew Jarvis and the Wingrave the kid wanted off him – this hassle that had *got* to be sorted. Or else how many nights would he end up sitting doing things like this stupid map again?

But, not many was the answer. Because Hard Stew wasn't out to *annoy* like this, he was out to *hurt*. He was violent; he broke arms – he'd been expelled from Junior School for doing a kid's radius in two places, only came back to Greenlands because the council cuts had closed all the special schools. Jarvis was out for blood – and there wasn't going to be any let-up till he'd proved his power and Davey had paid him his protection. With the Wingrave. Jarvis had to stay top man, what Grandad called "the guv'nor": and hadn't Jarvis let everyone know he *wanted* – and therefore he had to *have*?

But, the crunch of it was, *how* could Davey let him have the Wingrave? If it was down to him, he'd do it like a shot. He'd let him have the bike for Bell's asking price and forget the over-the-top money; just get himself something else: people always had fairish machines for sale at the Wheelers. Then he'd be free to go out and enjoy his riding again.

The trouble was, it wasn't down to him, it was

down to his dad – and John Booth would be most unhappy about that.

Although, hold on! *Hold on!* Thinking about riding out, wasn't there just a chance? Davey picked up his pen, and rested it again. Something was coming, something was starting to gell, something his dad *might* swallow ... Not some made-up reason about the Wingrave not being up to the mark, not some invented thing his grandad used to call *knock-kneed*, going on about it not riding as well as he'd thought, or the gears had the wrong ratios; or he was ready to move up a wheel size; nothing like that. But telling the truth ...

What had Davey Booth been doing this past two months since joining the Reach Wheelers? What had Stan Barrett got him doing, on top of the club runs? He'd been going out to Herne Hill velodrome, regular, to the banked racing track, borrowing the club's fixed-wheel bikes and racing in the under-sixteen events. Stan Barrett reckoned him to be a good wheel on the track and had got him his racing licence. And his grandad had been out to see him race, and so had his mum and dad. An Olympic sport.

So, why wouldn't his dad accept him wanting to go for that? Wouldn't his dad buy the idea that he'd rather have his own fixed-wheel *track*

machine? After a couple of weeks on the Wingrave
doing the road and circuit stuff, now he'd decided
he wanted to track-race for real, the serious stuff;
and he could always pick up a cheap mountain
bike for the day-to-day club rides.

Davey thought hard about it, and it seemed
ideal. And the same as before, he started to believe
it himself. He tested his dad's replies in his head,
and he didn't hear him coming up with more than
a "Strewth!" of surprise at this happening so soon.
No way did he hear an outright "No".

Which had Davey sitting up with a poker back.
Fellers, he'd got a result! Because Hard Stew *would*
win, he'd got to; he had to show he had the power –
and wasn't this the slickest way of just letting him?
The only other option was right off track – telling
his dad he was being bullied for the bike. Even if
the man didn't wave it away out of hand, even if he
went up the school or round to Mrs Jarvis, what
then? Would that vanish Hard Stew off the face of
the earth? Would it *not*! Jarvis wouldn't end up in
court and get taken down to serve a life sentence,
would he? No way. He'd just leave it a week before
making Davey's life hell again. He'd keep his
threats in spades, would Jarvis, he'd put Davey off
road *and* track for six months, and snort laughing
while the tossing world did nothing effective.

It was only Davey's grandad who had the sort of edge to him that Jarvis would have given respect to. Only Grandad would have made Jarvis know and believe what would happen if he didn't leave Davey alone. And Grandad was gone – no doubt stamping round heaven with the hump because he couldn't sort this villain out.

And, yes – heaven, not hell, thank you very much.

Davey got on with the map, but the line wouldn't flow; he was down again when he thought of Grandad in heaven, grief caught you like that; and wouldn't Uncle Cyril's poison always taste till he could spit it out of his mouth?

Fancy wishing someone like Sam Butler in hell! OK, no one was perfect. He wolfed his dinners, mashing everything up whatever it was, eating "uncouth", as Davey's dad called it. There were times when you could see a look in his eye which told you not to argue the toss with him; or you caught some jut of the mouth when he suddenly seemed like a man you didn't know. And sometimes he showed a real flash of temper – like when his new pension book wasn't in, or a driver cut him up on his bike. But none of that amounted to deserving hell fire, did it?

Davey shook his head; sat there and actually

shook his head, and looked up embarrassed in case his mum had seen him. But she was out in the kitchen, stacking the dishwasher and singing along with the *EastEnders* tune. Well, that was a treat. She hadn't done any singing round the house since before Grandad had been taken ill. Perhaps sorting the bungalow had helped? "Known and noted, done and done with", as the old man would have said.

Davey went to the kitchen and leaned on the fridge, watching her. In the last few weeks she'd been looking older than that photograph of her own mum, a few years up on the young Nan. But tonight she was back to being more Babs again than Barbara. For a start, she was in her summer shorts instead of her dark tracksuit trousers; and her white vest put her in a different league to her tight-to-the-neck black shirt. Her hair was undone and down with just a bright butterfly brooch at the back; and instead of her trainers she was in bare feet.

And Mum in bare feet was always a good sign. Before their holiday every year she always set about hardening up her soles for the hot Menorca sand. So bare feet was looking forwards – moving on – and a bit of hope.

"Mu-um . . ."

"Da-vey ..." Another good sign, her taking the rise.

"About Grandad ..."

"Yes?"

"Well, it's hard to say ..."

"So's taramasalata, but I still order it." Brave bluster. She shut the dishwasher door, pressed the button and turned round, stood looking at him, the back of her dishcloth hand to her eye. "With all his faults, we're going to miss the old devil."

"Yeah, I know. Which is what I'm trying to say. *How* was he an old devil?"

She didn't blink. "Davey, all old men are old devils. It's the way we talk about them – discounting the odd saint."

"Like Uncle Cyril?"

"Uncle Cyril? He's an old devil *royale*, that one – Old Nick himself! Now come on, that'll do; I'm busy – and so are you ..."

But she was wiping down what she'd wiped down only seconds before; all what his dad called *agitato*. Davey had rattled her perch, somehow.

"Did you know what Uncle Cyril said in the funeral car?"

Still she wiped, the same spot over and over. "No, I wasn't in it, was I? An' they didn't have car-to-car." To get away she snatched up an almost empty bunny bag from the swing bin and tied it up for the wheelie, total waste.

"He said he hoped Grandad went to blazes."

"The spiteful old beggar." She didn't give it the time of day, went to the back door with the bunny bag, swinging it, a sudden light touch. "Uncle Cyril and Grandad was never best mates; he's only come out of the woodwork for the last knockings. Forget it!" She tried the door but had to turn the key.

"Was he a good ol' dad, then? Grandad?"

"As they go, yeah, I suppose he was." Her voice was so airy-fairy she could have been Tinkerbell. But now she was leaning on the door handle, had a look on her face which said she was going to finish this off before she went outside. "I didn't see so much of him, to be honest. He spent a lot of time away when I was a girl ... working, trying to make us a better life."

"Where'd he go?"

"All over. Australia for a bit ..."

But Grandad had never talked Australia to Davey.

"Before Nan died or after?" There was mystery all over this.

"After."

"He went off *because* she died? Upset?"

40

"Yeah, that's about it." But Davey knew she was jumping at an easy answer.

"So how did she die?"

"Shortage of breath." As quick as you like. A get-out.

Now she went at the door handle like someone pulling the lever on a trapdoor. "Come on, get to that homework or you won't have it done by Christmas." And she stepped out into the garden, giving a yelp as she trod on something sharp.

Chapter Four

WEDNESDAY – WHEN Davey was going round to the bungalow that night come hell, high water – or Hard Stew. And how? He was going to do what he could have done with Claire: shoot the *wrong way* down Bardon Road and out into Paxwell Street where Jarvis wouldn't reckon to see him coming. A sprint down Thorn Hill and he'd be there – for a last walk round those rooms, a private sit in his grandad's chair, and a quiet talk to the old man's ghost with no one to cramp him.

This meant he was going to have to give Dan Brewer another freeze, even though they'd reckoned on having a cycle freak evening – talking specifications and road tests, reading the mags. Davey had a lot of time for Dan Brewer; they'd been best mates since primary school, gone on to the same comprehensive, were going to choose the same options. He was no fighter, Dan – a bit of a bottler, as it went – but he was a good wheel, and they always had a laugh.

With one eye out for Hard Stew – what changed? – and the other for Dan Brewer, Davey went into school. And there was Dan coming across the yard, waving a flap of paper.

"Got it, son; it's come!"

"Your marriage certificate?" Davey looked at the boy who called his bike "Ma Brewer" because he reckoned it was the nearest he'd ever get to being married to anything. Not bad-looking, Dan, a bit of a honk of a nose but it went all right with the helmet, the Tour de France touch.

"Application form for my licence."

"Yeah?" Davey already had his racing licence – you weren't insured to race without one.

Dan held up the form for Davey, as if he hadn't seen one.

Davey squinted at it. "Easy. 'Name' – you should manage that. 'Cycling club' ... Yeah, you can cope ..." Davey's trouble was, cycling was losing its edge for him these days.

"Do it tonight, eh? Round my place?"

Dear old Dan. Most times this would have been something to go for. Dan's mother thought people couldn't survive without crisps and Coke on the half-hour.

"I was gonna talk to you about tonight . . ."

"No, it can't be your grandad! Not now . . ." And you could see straight off that Dan wished he hadn't said that. "Sorry, mate."

But it had put Dan on the wrong side of the line, so the let-down came that bit easier. "We're still sorting stuff. I've *got* to be there. It's only this week; it all goes, Saturday."

Dan folded and filed the application form; side pocket of his Head bag. "I can manage. No bother spelling *solo*." And Dan drifted off; which might or might not have been due to Hard Stew coming on a Rottweiler walk across the yard.

And no time to get away.

"That bike, Boove."

"What about it?"

Jarvis pushed Davey's shoulder, hard. "You 'kin *know* what about it."

Davey looked round the yard. Coming up behind Jarvis was his little bunch of imitation hard men, all doing his walk, all wearing his poison-in-the-mouth face; one or two of them in older years, but age didn't come into things with Jarvis. Jarvis had the power; he could have been six and they'd still have stood there each side of him like bouncers at the door, showing loyal.

"That bike's mine, and I wan' on it? Right? No

44

questions, no tossin' around. My 'ouse wiv it, and you get the dosh. Which ain't stealin' nothin', it ain't *criminal* to pay the askin' price."

The firm sniggered at *criminal*.

But not Davey. "It's not down to me, Stew. It's down to my dad," he said. Which was true.

"Well, your dad can come, can't 'e? Bet my mum'd be chuffed to see 'im."

No snigger now. No one laughed at Jarvis's mother. Jarvis could *turn*.

"Listen, straight up, I'm going to do it, but I've got to work on him – my dad. Else he just won't let me."

Jarvis pushed his face closer; close enough for Davey to smell the breakfast he'd had from the Asian shop. "Then you work on 'im, or I'll work on *you*." Still face to face, Jarvis suddenly gripped the fingers on Davey's hand, bent them back, all one movement. "These only go so far, son, then they give. Snap like KitKats."

"Let go!"

Jarvis let go, but only to grab the other hand. "Those five, then these five." He bent the fingers of the left hand even further, millimetres off the break. "*When?*" he asked. Extreme pain.

"Half term," winced Davey. "I can't do it before, no bull."

"*Can't?*" Jarvis let go all but the long middle finger, concentrated on it.

"Can't not yet. But I will. Let go! *I will!* I've told you . . ."

Jarvis let go. He turned to his Loyals. "'E says 'e will! *An'* 'e will, you see!"

"Yeah, you *will*!" one of them added. And got a hard fist round the ear from Jarvis.

"'f I need a parrot, I'll go down the pet shop." And he led off into school, to have his way through the seven periods of the day.

Half-dislocated finger or not, Davey still shot the wrong way down Bardon Road later, sure he was going to make it. On account of what had gone off that morning, he reckoned he'd got half a lung of breathing space from Jarvis.

The Wingrave went like a dream. The Gripshift gears slid in and out with no jerk on the toe thrust, and already the Selle Royal Shock saddle felt as if it had been made to measure to the specifications of his backside. That was what gutted him – this bike was pure rock'n'roll.

So it wasn't the breeze that wet his eyes as he sped down Thorn Hill, it was the choking thought of parting with this beaut to Jarvis.

The brakes bit as he got to the bungalow. No

sign of Hard Stew – but Davey still wasn't hanging about out here, he was getting off the street quick. He'd nicked his mother's key from its little hook in the boiler cupboard – one of a dozen, it wouldn't be missed – so it was get in like a flash and lean the bike in the hallway.

Except that here came the old girl from the funeral, his grandad's neighbour, all smiles and "What are you doing here?" on her face.

"Hello, son."

"'Lo."

"You going in?"

"Yeah, doing a bit of sorting . . ."

"Saturday, is it, they're coming?"

"Yeah." Davey got as near as he could to the front door – as far as possible from sight of the road without seeming rude to the old girl.

"Taking the lot, are they?"

"'cept the carpets."

"Ah." The woman came round from her own side of the low privet hedge and put a hand on the gate latch. "I always admired that marble mantel clock, myself, every time . . ."

So that was her game! She was on the scrounge. "My auntie took that, Monday," Davey told her.

"Oh, well, good luck to her, it's hers by right."

47

The old woman retreated. But she was down about it, Davey could tell. "I'll let you get on."

"Cheers." Davey put the key in the door.

"And I don't care what anyone says, he was a gentleman, your grandad. One of the best."

"Yeah. Ta." And Davey let himself in to the Old Holborn smell he loved, which was fighting a losing battle this week with his mum's Dettol.

He put his bike against the passage wall and took off his lid and glasses, breathed in deeply, tried to savour his grandad's spirit. But the rooms were ready to go, and the place felt about as lived in as MFI: putting a word on it, *dead*.

Besides which, Davey suddenly felt all "lumpy" – something not right and you can't put your finger on it, dislocated or not. Something *done*, something *said*, something caught out of the corner of your eye. Something *wrong*.

He went to the kitchen, where what hadn't been wanted by the sisters was ready in cardboard boxes sitting on the oven top, which Grandad called "the hotplate"; his frying pan, the seat of all those happy sizzles; his cutlery, with their good cutting edges – "a bit of steel's a bit of steel, else you might as well be fitted up with plastic"; his tin teapot, in which he brewed "diesel" on the hour, marking the passing of the day; and tins and tins of soup which Auntie Glad was going to put aside for Harvest Festival at the school where she worked. And there was a full sack of rubbish for going out, on the top of which was Grandad's "snout tin" with its scratched Old Holborn lid. Davey grabbed it up, opened it, sniffed it; but the best of the smell had gone. It wasn't easy, bringing out his grandad's ghost. The only thing he could bring out was in his hand – the glass tankard with *DAVEY* painted on it. So why hadn't they thought he'd want to keep this?

He went into the living room for another try. In the middle stood the slim table with the drop leaves which came up at mealtimes, and two cardboard boxes of unwanted bits. Now Davey did what he hadn't wanted to do the other night. He rooted in them, and stood up shocked at what else they didn't want – Grandad's own stuff, his *personal* bits. Not his pension and policies, but his wallet and his reading glasses, and his watch – a solid Rotary, the battery still ticking round and giving the right time. Personal stuff they were going to get a price for off the second-hand man.

Now, staring at the watch, Davey *could* get a glimpse of his grandad. Those old blue eyes looking at the time, steadying it on his wrist between his thumb and forefinger as the one o'clock pips came out of the radio. And, "Gotcha!" he'd say, as if he were the SAS synchronising on a raid.

Well, he wanted Grandad's watch for himself, thank you! And why hadn't he been asked if he wanted it on Monday? Or anything else for that matter – them knowing how close "the chaps" had been? Because they hadn't. No one had wanted anything for themselves. From what was said, the stuff that had gone home on the seats of the cars was more for getting a better price than the second-hand man would give; none of it was stuck up in pride of place at Davey's. It was as if they'd been clearing out a stranger's pad.

Davey stroked the watch face down his cheek, looked at it, looked at his cyclist's digital on the other wrist; and "Gotcha!" he said. Too right, he'd ask for this on Saturday, before the man came.

So, was that what he'd felt lumpy about, them wanting nothing of his grandad's things – and him lying about it to the old girl? But somehow he didn't go for that.

He rooted around in the boxes a bit more. The playing cards, the poker dice – they'd all be nothing without Grandad's hands stroking them in a game – they could all go. But the penny whistle Davey wasn't so sure about. He picked it up, gave it a dry toot, nothing like his grandad with it, coming out with marching tunes.

"That's good!" Davey had told him. "You could give concerts."

"I oughta be warm at it! Twenny-three hours out o' twenny-four!"

And Davey had reckoned that had to be some practice to put in. But he could never bring back those tunes himself so he wouldn't ask for it.

He rooted some more; but there was nothing else. The watch would go on ticking and living, but the rest of this stuff would only remind him about his grandad *not* being here. Perhaps his mum and Auntie Glad had been right – most keepsakes and ashes in pots were sad items; what you needed to take on with you was the person in your head.

And that was the way he'd remember the special old gentleman who'd been Samuel George Butler. In his head, where it would never wear out.

A special old gentleman. That would be a fair description for the crematorium book. But why put it like that? Why was that in his head? He'd heard it tonight, hadn't he – what the old girl next door had said? "I don't care what anyone says, he was a gentleman, one of the best."

So, who said he *wasn't* a gentleman or one of

the best? Was there a coachload of people who all reckoned he ate a bit "uncouth"? Were there lines of noses turned up at some of his sayings? "A gentleman never calls a meat pie a 'whodunnit'!" All like his dad?

Was that the reason why Davey was feeling lumpy? He sat down in his grandad's armchair. Could be, he thought – because that made two remarks about Grandad not being all that. That one of Uncle Cyril's – and what the old girl had said.

He shut his eyes, tried to blank it all out, tried to fix on what was good – which was him doing what he'd planned to do, sitting in the chair which was the closest on earth to his grandad's ghost.

But no ghost came. He sniffed at the chair's covers, worn by the old man's head; he rubbed at its arms; but nothing. The spirit of Sam Butler had gone.

And still he felt lumpy.

He pulled himself out of the chair and wandered into the bedroom; his grandad's bedroom; and even now it was like going somewhere secret. It was always neat and *cold*, this room – on account of the window being forever open. It was a place Davey had rarely been offered into because Grandad was always up and about first; he slept like a flea. He'd kept the door mostly shut; but when Davey had seen inside he'd always thought it had to be like the army. The blankets on the bed were always boxed up as sharp as the woodwork round a top bunk, and there was nothing cosy. It always had a soldier's touch.

The room was even sparser today, after Auntie Glad had done the business: the bed linen gone, just the mattress, looking like a hospital bed waiting for a new patient. No pictures on the wall, and the mantelpiece empty except for one item. Nothing in there to say *which* old soldier had dreamed his dreams in these four walls.

Hang on! *Except for one item!* Davey reached over to the mantelpiece; and a flip of his heart told him there *was* something that was Grandad, as close to him as you like! He picked it up, switched it on: Grandad's night-time torch, the one he got up with in the dark, used with his bedtime "reader", and came in to fetch when there was a ferret on for something out in the shed.

And it still had a yellow glow left in the battery. Like with the watch, everything hadn't died.

Davey stroked the torch. He clicked it on and off and he heard his grandad clicking it on and off, sparing it – "Save it, mate, leave juice in the tank." Not a big rubber job like Davey's dad's but a flat shiny torch which took a four point five battery, with a thick round lens like half a clear sphere; a cyclops eye.

Well, maybe Auntie Glad hadn't wanted the torch; but Davey did. The sound of that old click had got him nearer Grandad's ghost than anything else; and wasn't a torch always useful? He slipped it in his pocket; no need to ask anyone for this, it wouldn't sell like the watch would.

He took a long last look round the room before going out; a final check; a last goodbye. He breathed in deep and sighed it out; he half closed his eyes and tried to see the bed made up again and the pictures back on the wall, those white beaches and blue sky – probably Australia from Grandad's years out there. He tried to see the bedside table with the torch on it and whatever "reader" Grandad had on the go. He tried to see the mantelpiece with the small marble clock the old girl next door had wanted.

And his eyes opened wide.

What he'd just seen in his head had been made up of *glimpses* over the years, no more – snaps through the crack of a door; this door which had been mostly shut because the room was Grandad's private place. And that clock had never sat anywhere other than on the bedroom mantelpiece –

not in line with the view from the door, not even through the crack.

Davey had gone so dry he had to swallow to get some spit. His stomach was rolling like empty. His face felt numb, like after a Jarvis smack. Because this changed everything. He'd always thought *he* was the main one; one of the two chaps. Special. Exclusive. The "oppo".

But for that old girl next door to know about it, she had to have been in here. In this private cell.

She'd *always* admired his marble clock, she'd said! And what else? *Every time!* Those were her words. Now, standing there, Davey knew for sure why he'd been feeling lumpy. His grandad had had the woman next door in here, regular!

He turned full circle and came back to stare at the empty mantelpiece. Well, there was nothing against that, was there? Grandad wasn't being a naughty boy, his Louise had died years before Davey was born, he was entitled to a bit of love and comfort if he wanted it.

But it wasn't the fact of what had gone on – the shock was the finding out that his grandad had that secret.

The shock of realising that he hadn't known his grandad nearly as well as he'd thought.

Chapter Five

SATURDAY – *SADDER-DAY*, the final clear-out. And did Davey imagine it, or were they pleased to be seeing the last of Grandad – all his belongings got shot of, nothing of the old man left behind? Or were the busy-busy-busy faces they had on just the way the two daughters coped? Because the way she ticked off stuff going out, Auntie Glad could have been clearing up after a jumble sale at her school. And Davey's mother had eyes as dry as a skeleton's, even when Grandad's chair went through the front door.

There was one plus – Uncle Cyril wasn't about, or they'd have had to hold Davey off decking him if he'd come out with any more of his remarks. But altogether it felt as if Davey were riding the wrong way to the rest of the pack; and made only worse by who else was there. Claire, with her hair up in bunches, eyes the same blue as Grandad's, clompy shoes and no socks, smooth legs, like something off a statue – one of those marble jobs you walked round a couple of times without wanting people to know what you were looking at. Claire, being Miss Helpful.

First off, she helped by wheeling out the Claud Butler. Davey was already twisted up about the bike – because wouldn't it have done him a turn if he sold the Wingrave to Jarvis and went for a track bike instead? He'd need something else for the road. But he hadn't dared raise it with his dad yet; this had all come too quick.

Davey had bagged the watch, though. He hadn't tossed around with Auntie Glad and a committee meeting; he'd taken it out of the cardboard box before the clearance men could start raking through it; "Mixed box, job lot, how much, missus?" – and he'd showed it to his mum.

"Can I have Grandad's watch? For best?"

She couldn't say no. If she'd said no it would have meant she should never have said yes to him ever coming round here, evenings and weekends. She knew how much Davey had loved him, so she couldn't deny it now that he'd gone.

At the nod he put his cycling digital in his pocket and pulled on the Rotary. He patted his other pocket where the bedside torch was, a new battery fitted. He'd brought it from home in case anyone missed it from the bedroom mantelpiece, then he wouldn't have to confess to coming here on Wednesday; he'd picked it up today, hadn't he?

He went to the living room and looked out at the van in the road, followed the heave of the disconnected cooker. The main curtains were down, but, like the carpets, the nets were being left, so the world couldn't see in. He stood and watched. He wasn't helping; he wasn't in the mood for doing the men's job for them; he just wanted to be here at the last knockings.

But there was Claire tripping out with a lampshade and getting a thank you from the main man as if she'd given him a golden crown to put upon his head.

And that strange taste came in Davey's mouth again; and he was breathing very shallow, as if a deep breath would make him snort out loud and show him up. She was a great girl, Claire! Pretty. Sparky. Classy. And couldn't he kick himself for being so pathetic over the bike ride last Monday?

Her taste in his mouth – and suddenly the taste of blood! Because who was walking cock-of-the-north past the bungalow? Only Jarvis! Stuart Jarvis on his own and staring in at what was going on.

Davey stepped back, did what his grandad did

when he was bossing out of the window at anyone. "Back, out of the throw of light! Always get yourself a yard back." Action Man talk.

Davey saw Jarvis looking at the stuff in the van, staring in again at the bungalow. And he thanked God he'd come here in his mum's car, hadn't left the Wingrave out at the front.

Not that Jarvis would have seen any bike right now. He'd seen Claire, on her next trip with a couple of cushions, and Claire wasn't the sort you looked past.

Jarvis stood like *rooted*, and spat on the pavement.

Claire passed him and went to the van, threw the cushions in before coming back. She hadn't given Jarvis a look. Or hadn't seemed to.

"Tha's it, throw 'em away."

Claire blanked him.

"You don' need cushions, babe. Not wi' them froopenny bits!" And he made one of those obscene Rottweiler yelps, the caveman's love call, grabbing his own chest with two hands.

Davey's blood boiled in his throat, he couldn't breathe. He stood even further back as Jarvis came to the gate and watched Claire right the way into the house, heard him do a final yelp. But in case Claire caught him watching as she came past the living room, Davey threw himself down to the fire on the wall and pretended to check that it was dead.

She went straight through as if nothing had happened. She didn't come running in to her mother, didn't break step. Well, Davey reckoned, a pretty girl like her, she probably got that sort of thing all the time. And he felt so jealous it hurt.

He watched Jarvis lurch off on his leering way as Claire came into the living room.

"*Anything* else to do?" she asked, that lilting way of speaking that Davey heard in his head, nights.

"No."

She turned to go out again.

"But there's this, to keep." Davey didn't know what he was doing, he just was; he was pulling his grandad's torch from his pocket.

"What's that?"

"Mum gave it to me," he lied. "Grandad's special torch." He held it on the flat of one hand, like something precious, gleaming where he'd polished it.

"*Very* nice."

"For you. You have it. They're handy, and ... it'll put you in mind of Grandad."

"Oh." Claire took the torch, held it on her palm

60

the way Davey had done, and then put her other hand on top, rubbing it slowly with her fingers as if a genie might appear. "I'd *like* it. Thanks."

And dreams did come true. Sometimes. Never mind stuck up a tree in Oxleas Wood, there and then in Grandad's living room Claire leant forward and kissed Davey thank you – just a brush of lips, but a kiss. A voluntary, unnecessary kiss – and on the mouth! And if anyone had asked Davey a question just then, he'd have answered like a cassette on fast forward . . .

"Right, that's it!" the clearance man shouted from the front door. Outside, a loud bang said the van was being shut on Grandad's stuff. The man came through into the kitchen, where Auntie Glad was standing at the work top with a calculator and her notebook.

She showed him the final sum. "Is this what you say?"

He went down his own scrap of paper, hieroglyphics and round pounds.

"Twenny off for cash . . .?"

"No, I'll take a cheque for the full amount."

The man didn't argue. He pulled out a wad of money from his trouser pocket and counted out the full amount. Auntie Glad made him sign her book, and she signed his paper. And he went, nothing else said.

Davey hurried back into the living room to see the van go; but the driver must have been reversing it in the side road because it wasn't there any more. Well, he was spared the wrench he'd had when the cremation curtains had pulled across. He took in a deep breath, looked round the room. Nothing here any more. Apart from his watch and Claire's torch, Grandad had gone.

Davey made a point of checking the time on the Rotary, and went back to the kitchen, where his mother was stuffing her half-wad into her pocket.

Auntie Glad dangled the front door key. "I'll drop this into the Town Hall."

"Ta."

Claire had locked the back door and was hanging the key on its nail. She smiled at Davey, a consoling smile, as if to say she knew the way he had to be feeling. He smiled a brave smile back.

"Banging shut another door," said Auntie Glad.

"Yes," said Davey's mum. "No good looking back."

"Nothing to look back on," Auntie Glad replied. She turned to Claire. "You're lucky," she told her, as they all made their way to the front. "We never had a father to look up to."

What had she meant by that? Davey's bedroom ceiling didn't have the answer. Did Auntie Glad mean Grandad hadn't been around to be a dad in those years when he was in Australia, trying to make money for them to have a better life? Because you could look up to someone who did that, whether they were at home or not. Kids could still look up to fathers who'd gone off for years to fight in a war, whether they came back or not. Davey didn't know – and he wasn't going to ask again, not yet. He'd let his mother's grieving take a few more weeks, he didn't want to worsen wounds that hadn't healed. But he'd remember.

Anyway, he'd got his own sweet pain to bear today. And it *was* a pain; it was so real it hurt, that jealous feeling that anyone else might even know Claire, might be talking to her this minute, seeing her over the weekend, sitting in the same form room as her next Monday. But it was a pain he was glad to have; *because he'd got reason for having it.* She'd kissed him, on the lips, she'd forgiven him for being a hobbit over the cycle ride. It seemed like they were back to where they'd been in the shed, with her on the Claud Butler. When Auntie Glad had driven off today, Claire hadn't sat there staring out of the far window like before. Today she'd shouted, "*See* you, cousin!" And the little nod she'd given with the flash of her eyes, had said she meant it. Which gave him so sweet a pain that he wanted it never to go away: a pain that had driven him to look up Auntie Glad's and Uncle Richard's number in the address book, and say it over and over till he could get to his bedroom and write it down. Because when he'd got another bike after Jarvis had got the Wingrave, he'd ring her, and ask her out. There was plenty of summer to come. They could sit together in Gerry Gelato's. They could leave their bikes and go for a walk in Oxleas Wood. He could hold her hand and help her over fences. And he went to sleep that Saturday night seeing her face, and saying her name over and over until it became a nonsense. A sweet pain of nonsense.

It was a Sunday, and the Reach Wheelers were on a club run to Vigo Village, via Eynsford. Meeting up at Bexley station, they were taking the B roads to Crockenhill, then following a familiar route to Davey because he'd cycled it with Grandad on his Claud Butler – twisting along between high hedges and over the M25 to freewheel down the side of the Darent Valley to the river at Eynsford. The rule being, pairs on the wider roads, single file on the lanes.

Dan Brewer was there with Davey, there was a pack of others who all knew each other – and Claire, who had also joined the club. And it was a golden day. Davey and Claire were partnered off, Claire leading when they went to solo on the run-down through the steep lanes, and Dan Brewer not seeming to mind being on his own so long as he was in front; the birds were singing in the bushes on either side, and the road was humming under the whir of twenty pairs of wheels.

Down to the green at Eynsford for a rest on the grass, a drink from their bottles, and a paddle in the ford; and the usual dares given out as to who would wade the water carrying their bike, instead of riding over the narrow hump-backed bridge.

They looked at the ford from the green, that exciting splash through for coaches and vans with high axles, and for cars when the Darent was running low. A large vertical ruler between the bridge's twin arches showed the depth of water, nearly two feet today.

And there was Claire, sproncy Claire, paddling deeper than the others, over to the first of the two arches.

"Don't fall over!" Davey called.

"Would you miss me if I floated off like Ophelia?"

"Nah!" Davey lay on the grass, sucked on his water bottle, next to Dan Brewer for the old friendship, but keeping an eye on Claire, who was venturing under the arch. It was dark under there, and she was shining Grandad's flat torch at the old grey stones.

When, "Do you mind!?" she shouted.

Davey raised himself up and squinted into the dark under the bridge. There was someone in there, barring her way.

"Hard Stew Jarvis!" said Dan Brewer, stopping his wiping of spokes.

And it was! Stuart Jarvis was blocking Claire and pulling his mouth wide with a finger from each hand, waggling his tongue at her like some obscene frog.

"Gi's a kiss!" he said.

"Drop dead!" said Claire. "Sooner kiss our cat's backside!"

Davey started tearing at his cycle shoes and socks, but somehow slowly. He stared at Jarvis under the bridge.

"What's going on?" he asked Dan Brewer.

"He's got her where he wants her, that's what!"

And before Davey could get into the water and wade over – he was so slow, as if something were holding him back – Stuart Jarvis had pressed

Claire against the stone arch, bending the fingers back on both her hands to stop her resisting, and was kissing her, hard on the mouth.

Claire was trying to push him back, twisting her head this side and that, which only seemed to please Jarvis, and she couldn't shake him off until he decided to stop, and let her go with a slap on her bottom, wading off laughing downstream, spitting into the water, and carrying Davey's Wingrave held high above his head like cyclo-cross.

Claire pulled a cushion from Grandad's out of her cycling top and threw it at Jarvis. It splashed short, and he yelped at her.

Too late, Davey got to Claire. "Which way'd he go?"

She was spitting out herself. "Where do you think? Down there." She looked at Davey, disappointed, let down. "Go on, hobbit! Get him, then!"

Davey stared – at where Jarvis had stopped in midstream and was giving him the come-on to fight.

When with a huge effort, like dragging himself up the side of a crumbling pit, Davey deliberately woke himself up before he had to take the bully on.

In a sweat, dribble on his pillow, breathing

hard, heart racing for real like the end of a five-lap scratch, Davey stared up into the dark and said a thank you to God that it had all been in his head. But he was cursing himself for not being man enough to take on Stuart Jarvis, even in his dreams. And he lay there hoping like hell that the other people in dreams don't have them, too – because how could he ever face Claire after that performance.

Worse, it asked the serious question as to what he would do if that story ever came true. And the answer brought him down; because he reckoned he wouldn't do anything different.

Underneath, Davey Booth was nothing but a cringing little coward.

Chapter Six

WHY WAS Eynsford so in the front of Davey's mind? Why go there in his sweaty dreams? The Reach Wheelers had regular runs all over – so was it because he'd been there with his grandad, enjoying his mountain bike, pedalling fast after the old man, whistling downhill and leaning round the twisting lanes?

Was it the memory of lying on that patch of green by the river, that first real touch of the country outside "the smoke"? "Used to dream of all this when I couldn't have it," Grandad had said. And Davey had been content to watch the lorries splash through the ford and send waves up the strand; and happy as Larry the day a car got stuck when the water was too deep.

The truth of it was, Eynsford was *happy*, it was their place, it summed up "the chaps" a treat. So this week, with his grandad gone, it had to be strong in his head.

That particular Saturday they'd lain there sucking grass and watched this Nissan Primera going in all speed and show, a spotty exec at the wheel and a girl up front; and he nearly made it, got to within two metres of the other side – *Please test your brakes* – but the car stopped those two metres short. The engine died with a splut as the water got into the electricals and the car's wash calmed like pond water lapping round an old shopping trolley.

"Hobbit!" It tickled Grandad. "That's the biggest idiot thing to do in the world – take on what you've never sussed."

It was only feeling sorry for the passenger that got Grandad to his feet and peeling off his shoes and socks, rolling up his tracksuit bottoms.

"Come on, boy," he said, "'the chaps' to the rescue. Let's give matey a lifeboat." But they let matey get his feet wet first, giving the girl a piggy-back out, before they helped him push the car clear of the ford.

The spotty exec took his tissues to the spark plugs, while the girl took Davey and Grandad back across the bridge for a thank you pint and a bar of "nutty". And that was it, Grandad was all for downing it quick and off on their saddles. But didn't he choke on his shandy when the pub's

70

guv'nor came out? The bloke came into the beer garden for empties, took one look at Grandad and put down his pots.

"Strewth!" he said, "Sammy Butler."

Davey twisted to see Grandad's face. He'd never heard him called Sammy before – it made him sound younger, like someone else.

"Jack Lee!" said Grandad. They nodded at each other; didn't shake hands. The man was about Grandad's age with tight grey hair close to his head, tall, thin, with bony fingers.

"My grandson." And the guv'nor shut his mouth on whatever he was going to say next. "Hang up your truncheon, Jack?"

"Don't fret, Sammy – I've still got it on its hook down behind the bar."

"Good for you."

They both laughed; but before any more chat a bell rang to call the guv'nor into the bar.

And they drank up, Davey taking the lead from Grandad and downing his fast, while the girl was going on about other berks she'd known in her time.

"Our beat copper, Jack was," Grandad told Davey over a fry-up that night. "Out of Downham. One of the old school, very fair, straight goer. Kept us all in good order with a cuff round the lug and a kick up the jacksie."

And Davey thought how great it must have been in the olden days, when your run of streets was a bobby's beat, and you knew them by name and felt a bit protected. He could do with a Jack Lee round his streets right now, with the likes of Jarvis ruling them the way he did ...

Except that a Jack Lee could sometimes make life hell as well as heaven.

At uplift time, school Assembly, last thing in the afternoon on the Monday, Davey stood in line with Dan Brewer to croak through the Southampton hymn – 'For All the Saints'. A short sermon from the head, notices, and they could pick up their bags from the heaps in the corridor and scuffle off home – Davey still thinking he'd bought Jarvis off for a couple of weeks. But can the cat resist flicking at the mouse?

Jarvis and his Loyals were in line behind Davey and Dan. There was no reason why Davey should reckon there'd be any bother; but then, Jarvis always had to be gaining respect. Today, he talked racism through the hymn, had a laugh, dropped a gob on the hall floor, and then fixed on Davey.

"Don' you let me down, Boove! I don' like 'kin traitors!"

With Jarvis's voice coming at him, Davey had to let him know it was going to be sorted. Like he'd said, he'd got a plan and he was working at it – which is what he could have told him in the yard or the corridor. But in the school hall he was too tucked up for that. He turned his head and nodded a bit, but that wasn't good enough for Jarvis. His Loyals couldn't see the respect without hearing the crawl.

"Boove!" Jarvis didn't bother with lowering his voice. Mr Carruthers, the head, was just going into his lean on the lectern and his, *You know, I often ask myself* ... touch; except Jarvis's voice made him take a quick shot in that direction.

But Jarvis, sure-fire certain no one would pull him, had to hear Davey's word. Out loud. This was *his* religion; down here he was holding *his* Assembly for the Loyals, and he wasn't going to leave off till he had his alleluia. He grabbed forward and pinched Davey's backside hard with the tough corrugated nails of a middle finger and thumb.

"Ow!" yelled Davey. He couldn't help it, it was the shock as well as the hurt – a loud shout that fell in one of those moments when the world was waiting for the head's crucial moral message.

The whole school turned, most laughed; Davey

went turkey and Jarvis stayed grinning, while the Loyals went down as if Billy Connolly was in town.

It was no good Davey turning his shout into a bad cough – already Jack Lee was on his way. Not Grandad's Jack Lee, of course, but the firm and fair, straight goer of a new PE teacher, Mr Julien. In his tracksuit and towelled neck, his strong black scrum-half's face frowning at this disorder, he came bombing along the line of Davey's year – with Davey already putting up his hands to the outrage.

The head had seen Mr Julien moving to deal with the disturbance and was trying to pick up where he was in his sermon. But there was no attention on him. Everyone in the hall was waiting to see Davey hoicked out and marched to the corridor for due punishment.

But, blow everyone down, Mr Julien hadn't come for Davey. He'd dropped a line behind and come steaming along the Loyals. It was Jarvis he was after.

"I saw what you was doin'! You gave that lad a nippin'!" He stood eye-balling Jarvis, who was doing his Category A insolent stare. Obviously the man wasn't up with Jarvis's reputation – no doubt on account of never turning up for PE. "Out! Wi' me!" Mr PE pointed a straight arm at the rear door; no mistaking, he was going for broke.

Mr Carruthers shut his eyes as if in prayer, and other staff looked at one another with those invisible shakes of the heads. *Bad mistake, showing out* – he'd have to learn, the new man.

And Jarvis was standing his ground. *You an' who's army?* said the body language.

"You hear me? I said 'Out!'" Now Mr Julien had taken the Assembly over; the sermon had stopped. Law and order, right and wrong, the downfall of the bully, the meek inheriting the earth, this was the moral agenda right now. No one's eyes or minds were anywhere else but on Mr PE and Public Enemy Number One.

Would Jarvis go? Was this to be the first split in his bullet-proof vest? Did the good guy win, or the bad guy?

He didn't move a muscle, except to wipe off his smirk for a cold, hard stare. *Make me!* his eyes said.

And Mr Julien was about to. His arm came up to grab at Jarvis's shoulder, which brought back the smirk at the thought of the assault charge to come.

But Mr Carruthers suddenly found the gift of tongues. "Leave it, Mr Julien! He's not worth the trouble." And Mr Julien, after a look to check, had to leave it, but not without the last word.

"Gymnasium A, tomorrow morning nine o'clock!" he said, and strode back to his place – to hear the end of the head's uplifting message, all about cherishing hope in a hopeless world.

Now Davey saw his chance to turn round to Jarvis. "Couldn't help it. Sorry, mate," he said.

"You 'kin will be!" Jarvis came back. Which was riveted in Davey's mind as he scooped up his bag after Assembly and ran home fast, the long way round.

So why do something stupid like tripping out on the Wingrave that evening? Was everything so bad that it was some suicide Davey was into, just to get it over with? No way – Davey hated the sight of blood too much for that. It was just that in all this darkness he did have one hopeful beam of torch-light – and her name was Cousin Claire. Result, result, the girl had taken a shine to him, she'd given him a pain he loved having, on the soft side of things she made him feel sorry for everyone in the world who wasn't Davey Booth. So, in the depths of his "down" why not have a bit of the "up"? That was why he was getting out his bike, doing his wrong way ride down Bardon Road again. He was going over to Claire's streets out Bromley way, in the hope of accidentally bumping into her. That was what was driving him. He might even ring Auntie Glad's bell and ask for a glass of water! Because, what was life otherwise – nothing but homework, fretting, mooning about the house, and stupid nightmares.

Davey didn't dwell. He took his chances and he went, kitted for a proper ride-out – lycras, "hand of bananas" helmet, water bottle, clipless shoe plates, all that.

But the trouble with a trick like riding the wrong way down Bardon Road was, other people came up it the right way. And who did it have to be coming up tonight? Only Stuart Jarvis!

Had God gone on holiday?

Jarvis wasn't carrying a sign saying he was on the look-out for Davey; and he always had the same hard front on his face, so he *could* have been just out for the breeze. But Davey didn't reckon it. Jarvis wasn't a cyclist; he *had* a bike, like he had other things to show off his power by the having of them; he had a computer which he couldn't get into; but he'd no more put himself through the pain of a long run than he'd take up with the Thames Reach Morris Men. And his bike proved it all. What he was on was his mangled bike done up, but it was more *restored* than done up; it was smart, it was style. And it underlined what Davey knew – he only wanted the Wingrave for the having of it.

Bardon Road wasn't that steep; even so, Jarvis was up out of the saddle, hands on the bars instead of down on the ends, spooky eyes all round him. And as Davey came scooting down on the pavement, Jarvis saw him – and straight off, even worse than shouting his name, he hoiked the bike round and put himself on the chase. Out for the silent kill.

Davey forgot scooting, he threw his leg over the saddle, swerved round a man coming up, made it into Paxwell Street to a hoot from an angry Escort. With his head down into the sprint, he gripped up through the gears and swerved in and out of the traffic like a pursuit handicap, legs pumping as fast as they did on the banking at Herne Hill.

And Jarvis still wasn't shouting *"Stop!"*, still wasn't chucking mouthfuls of filth telling Davey how far behind he was. It was worse than any hare and hounds, being out in front with no sign as to how he was doing.

And what else Davey didn't know was how he was going to get back home in one piece. He could sprint a circuit round the district like Chris

Boardman, and still find Jarvis sitting on the end of his road, waiting.

Which left nothing for it but to go. He was fitter than any Jarvis when it came to cycling and he had got to make that count – because he was well weaker in any other way. He had to get some air between him and the hard man.

And straight off the first obstacle flew at Davey: a red light at a junction you couldn't mess with. Jarvis was one thing, a six-axle lorry was another. Which meant dismounting, losing time pushing his bike round the corner – no chance of crossing over – but at least he'd get a quick look back.

And, dogs' mess, there was Jarvis still coming, tighter than he'd thought, getting a pull off a drop-tail van.

Carrying, Davey swung his bike round into the dual carriageway, jumped on it again; his foot missing its hold but getting it second time, and it was head down again for the crank of his life – with Jarvis knowing he'd taken a left.

He raced on towards the Granada roundabout – what else could he do to get away, if Jarvis was keeping up in the traffic? – when suddenly a half-chance threw itself at him. A run of Grandad talk, in his head: *Surprise, mate; surprise, do the unthinkable.* Like someone jumping out of a shower when all that's in your head is which shampoo, or hiding *over* the door when they're expected to be behind it. And there was just a half-chance he could pull one.

The traffic was tight down here, always was, but there was a gap behind him from the change of the lights; and a gap here was rare; the stuff was always nose to tail and *moving* down this stretch towards the big junction.

So could he use that gap?

He had to! He gripped sudden and hard on his brakes, jumped off his bike, and – all one movement – vaulted the pavement handrail and pulled the bike over, running back up the road the way he'd just come.

And there was Jarvis pounding down tight between a bus and a long loader, no more chance of stopping sharp than joining the school choir.

He swung his head and saw Davey but he had to go on, he had no option, swearing atrocity. While Davey shot down an alley between the flats and into the web of streets that lay behind.

But where now? He still had no safe destination. He'd lost sight of Jarvis, but the kid could come at him from anywhere; and home was no-go for a couple of hours. While any chance of going to Claire's run of streets was blown right out.

So Davey pulled his last surprise: something he hadn't even thought about until that second. Head still down, checks at every corner, he didn't relax until he'd cut an arc across the circle of Thames Reach, through the estates, and came to the side road which led down past the back of the pensioners' bungalows: to the rear of his grandad's empty place.

A yelp of the brakes and he threw himself over the fence at the back and tucked his bike well in under the hedge. And with one wrench at the shed door he was inside it and finger-nailing the shortened bolt from the upright, to slide out the secret front door key.

He stood in the silent space and drew cool air into his hot lungs, blew it out in brief relief. Because he knew that Stuart Jarvis couldn't get at him in Grandad's empty bungalow. He didn't even know about the place . . .

Chapter Seven

IT WAS a cinch for Davey, Grandad's emergency plan. He pulled out the bike from under the hedge and ran it into the shed, wedged the door shut, and dodged round the side of the bungalow into the porch, where he slid the oiled key into the lock. Sorted!

Closing the front door fast behind him, he took more deep breaths in the hallway and shut his eyes. He was a fit animal, cycle pursuits were no shock to the system, but the scare of Jarvis had pumped him up like an Olympic finalist. Now he had to come down, relax on safe ground. He leant against the wall in the empty bungalow till his breathing was back to normal, opened his eyes and looked around. There was still nothing of his grandad here any more – except for the familiar swirl of his carpet and the shimmer of the net curtains.

He went into the living room and, keeping back

from the window again like one of the chaps, he stared out at the road in front. Thank God, no sign of Jarvis on the prowl – but even if there had been, he felt safe enough; Jarvis wouldn't think for a second that he'd be hiding in here. So it was sit on the carpet and give Jarvis's patience an hour to drain off before sneaking back home.

And sitting there without even the tick of a clock, it dawned on Davey that he hadn't been this still and quiet for ages. At home he was never alone unless he went to his room, and then it was homework or Sega or a mouse click round some of his games. And when he put out his light he'd lie on his bed and think about Jarvis and the bike, or the sweet pain of Claire, or the sadness of no more Grandad and what people were saying; but it would be dark, and sleep usually took him off quickly. Here in the bungalow there were no distractions, and no way was sleep on the menu.

He looked at his cycling watch. Ten past six. Well, he'd give it to a quarter to eight, and then he'd go; and, after tonight's fright, when he got indoors, he'd straight off start the Wingrave campaign. Because he couldn't go on like this. This Jarvis thing was going to come to a right bloody end. He'd get on to his dad and push hard with how he wanted to specialise in track racing – for

which he wanted a track-racing bike with something like an oval-tubed Columbus frame and
aero-rimmed high-pressure wheels, twenty-seven
inch, like the best of the club bikes he'd been
borrowing. And his dad *had* to see the logic in
that. You couldn't use the Wingrave for track
racing – and hadn't his mum and dad enjoyed
those mini Olympic events out at Herne Hill, with
a race commissar and the lap bell ringing? It was
so logical it had to swing through.

In his dreams! Davey stared at the floor – his
stomach rolling at the thought of facing his dad.
Davey wasn't a facer, he was a besider. He bet
Claire could do it, with all her up-front ways: but
her sort of style wasn't his. Him, he'd mumble and
blush and have *LIAR* as good as tattooed on his
forehead. He could never kid a cat he'd got a
mouse behind his back. Who was always first out
at games like Bluff?

He slid down the wall and sat resting his head
on the wallpaper, pictured Claire giving it some in
her sproncy way, not batting an eyelid while she
was at it. She'd get the bike changed and sell you
shares in Herne Hill before you could sit your
backside on a chair. She'd go at it the Grandad
way: attack, attack, attack. It was weird how they
were both grandchildren of the same man, and she

had some bits of him, and he had others. She had his *style*; black knickers for his funeral, this year's fruity colours for Saturdays; hair always pretty enough for the front of *Smash Hits*. Just like Grandad, who wouldn't go out of the house unless he was "suited and booted", even to have his hair cut. "Always look the 'daddy'," he'd say, "and you *are* the top man. Look a 'hobbit' and they'll make you a deficient."

That's what Claire had got off the old man – the style and the "front". So what had Davey got? He had to think about that; what it was that he was proud of being. And as he sat on the living-room carpet that he'd lain on so often, playing draughts or poker dice, his head leaning on the wallpaper he'd helped his grandad choose, Davey reckoned it was his knack for being a mate, a good listener, one of the team. And Grandad had been all those things, too: he always heard you out, always had the time to take an interest, always put himself ready to go along with you. "Right on, mate, that's what we'll do ..." – the two of them the chaps, musketeers, oppos.

He smiled at the thought of it. His special old grandad! And found himself with tears in his eyes to go with the smile on his lips.

And to go with the ache in his backside! It was

dead uncomfortable sitting here! He lifted himself and felt underneath, ran his hand over the carpet where it met up with the wall. Hard and lumpy – it felt like sitting on a wallet in your back pocket.

He lifted up and looked. And saw that he *had* been sitting on something. Grandad's carpet had come from Auntie Glad's when he'd moved in here, and now Davey saw something that hadn't shown with furniture in the room – that the carpet was a bit too big, and instead of cutting a foot or so off the side, it had been sewn over to make a flat seam all the way along, in case it was ever needed again. A flat, empty seam – except for the lump where Davey was sitting.

And there was something under there. Definitely, something. It wasn't big, only a little hillock in the swirl of the carpet; but it was there sure enough.

So, what was it? His grandad had never talked about anything in here when he'd told him the secret of the key in the shed – but then he hadn't told him about the old girl next door, either . . . Was it along those lines, then? Something *private* – like the sorts of things kids hid in their bedrooms, things they wouldn't want their mums to find?

That same bad feeling from the other night came over him again, the not knowing his grandad as well as he'd thought.

This little lump he hadn't known about was only an arm's length from the corner, probably handy for his grandad reaching it; and when Davey pulled at the carpet it came up a treat, with the carpet tacks laid loose in their holes.

He lay down and wriggled his hand in, like his dad getting to an awkward nut under the car. And a sudden scary thought – Grandad wouldn't have had reason to put a mouse trap under here, would he? *Nah!* All the same, the fingers that went in were more like a burglar's feeling their way in the dark than a shopkeeper's grabbing an item out of a fridge. Definitely trembly.

It was paper he touched, felt like an envelope, medium sized, well used, all soft edges; and as he pulled it out Davey saw that he was right, one of those brown manila jobs, not over stuffed, just the one item in it. He sat on the floor and drew it out. It was nothing rude, but some sort of official book. It was a car log book, an old one from the days when they really were books, with pages to show the changes of owner. And this was for a Vauxhall Victor DJJ 343, bought off Rowley Motors of Peckham. With just the one page filled in – which meant that Samuel George Butler had been its first and last owner.

And Davey's back tingled. Was *that* what stupid Uncle Cyril had been on about? Had Grandad crashed this car and killed someone? Was that why he was an old devil?

But Davey soon forgot all that – when he turned to the back cover and saw what the book was really for, protecting what was tucked into it: a black and white picture of a crowd of blokes and a couple of girls at the seaside, the photographer *Arnolds of Margate*. Everyone was smiling at the camera all Jack-the-lad with their arms round each other's shoulders. One of the girls – in a blouse and long skirt – was standing at the side not cracking her face, nose a bit out of joint. But the other girl was in the middle next to someone who had his arm round her waist – both looking like cats who'd got the cream.

And who else was the feller, but Grandad! Years back. And who else was the girl but a young Nan, looking like a film star. A hot day in Margate – with sunshine still smiling out of these two, even after all those years.

It was the sort of picture you had to grin at, no helping yourself. And the way you do, Davey made up the story: the lads on a beano who've met up with these two girls; and the usual touch, one up for it, one not – but because of the one who *was*, this was a picture of when Davey's grandad had met the girl he married; and a picture to make the world feel jealous. As he sat there staring at it, Davey's mouth started filling again with the taste of thinking about Claire.

But there was something on the back of the photograph, something faint, something other than the photographer's name. It was an address written in smudged Biro, but he could just make it out: *Louise Freeman, 128 Farquhar Road, Crystal Palace*. And Davey had a good idea what that was. It was Nan's address as a girl; Grandad had got it off her to make sure he met up with her again.

And that was the sort of "front" it took; knowing what you wanted, and going for it. His grandad had had it, in aces. And Davey made up his mind, right there and then, that he was going to have it too. That "front" was one of the things he was going to make sure he carried forward himself. The Rotary watch he'd already got; a touch of the young Sam Butler was what he was going to inherit, too.

He knew Claire's address, the same as his grandad had known his nan's. Since he'd found it in the phone book he'd gone round reciting it, like a religious chant. *37 Southlands Drive, Bromley,*

Kent. And he'd looked it up in the *A–Z* because if ever he'd been there as a younger kid, he couldn't have found the way these days. Now he knew it by heart, he'd cycled it in his daydreams, and he'd been heading for it for real tonight when Stuart Jarvis had shown. So what the hell was Davey Booth waiting for, lurking in here in the bungalow like a man on the run? Where was the "front" in that? Would Grandad have hung about on the back of a scare? One look at the beautiful girl in the picture, one thought of the beautiful Claire, and he had the answer to that.

Fired up, Davey couldn't backtrack to the shed fast enough. He pocketed the key to the front door and stuffed the envelope into his top. He hit the road in seventh gear to get out to Bromley as fast as he could, heading out of the circle of Thames Reach. Past the first couple of turnings there wasn't much chance of Jarvis looking for him in that direction. But having the front meant taking the chance.

He kept up a good speed with his head down, and before long he crossed the green of Chislehurst Common and rode into Bromley South.

The houses were bigger here, built in their own grounds, double garages as common as lampposts, and rough private roads to show how they didn't depend on the council. And this was where Claire lived . . .

Davey slowed a bit, with the feeling that he was getting out of his depth: these weren't the sort of London streets where you wouldn't be noticed wheeling up and down. And it was all so *posh*. He cruised, half a mind to turn round and head back home. But he was so close to Claire's, he might as well get a quick look at it. It wasn't this road, nor this next one, it had to be the turning after . . .

Southlands Drive. And the sight of the name on the sign sent Davey's inside into a flip. *Southlands Drive!* He pulled into the kerb and pretended to adjust his shoe plate, eyed the houses up and down the wide road. And he knew straight off that he'd wasted his time. There was no way he'd see Claire out here. These people didn't nip out of their houses; she wouldn't be popping down to the corner shop for a carton of milk. For a start, they didn't stoop to corner shops . . .

All the same, he told himself, on his way off out of it, he'd just take a quick look at number thirty-seven, just *see* where she lived. No harm in that. Slowly, he pedalled along Southlands. Plane trees grew tall and leafy on either side, over driveways wide enough for coaches. Some of the houses had names painted on fancy boards or chiselled into their gates, nothing so common as numbers. But Davey was delighted to see that Claire's wasn't one of those. A plain *thirty-seven* in writing was nailed to a tree; nothing poncy like "Beechwood Copse" next door.

He didn't know what Claire's dad did for a living; but he had to be making a fair screw, going by this place. With Auntie Glad's school money coming in it paid for a big old pad – traditional, squarish, small red bricks, and a conservatory almost as big as Davey's house. Auntie Glad's car was in the driveway, with more than enough room for another when Uncle Richard came in. Making Davey feel as much at home as a sparrow in an aviary. If he'd had any mad idea of knocking for a glass of water, he could forget that! There was no way he was going cold into this posh house.

He looked at his watch. By the time he got home Jarvis would be swilling Coke in front of some brain rot on the box; that scare was over – for tonight. Tomorrow at school would be different, but by then Davey could well have some news about the Wingrave. Patting the picture in his top, he still had his grandad's front to have a go with his dad when he got in. He'd got to – he *had* to get started on it sometime.

He pushed off. A couple of schoolkids in blazers

were coming along the pavement towards him; her in a boater, him lugging a sportsbag and a violin: and already they were eyeing Davey up as if he might be a blagger. There was that frowny look of the boy's face, and the perk of the girl's nose. Davey put on a spurt – and then the brakes.

The girl's nose? Only Claire's! The girl was his cousin, disguised in her school uniform. Davey wobbled, nearly came off.

"*Well!*"

"Hiya!"

"*What* are you doing here?"

"Cycling," he said – as daft an answer as you'd ever get: when the new up-front Davey should have said, "Looking for you!"

The boy with Claire had one of those looks on which usually come before either a shake of the hand or a punch on the nose. The kid turned to Claire, as if he were saying *Is he all right?* – but tons too polite to give it word.

"My cousin," said Claire.

And Davey didn't like the way the boy relaxed, either. So him being Davey Booth hadn't triggered off some raging jealousy; which told him she hadn't been going to school drooling over this fabulous cousin she'd met.

"Grandpa doesn't live here," Claire said.

"Grandpa?"

"My *other* Grandpa – *your* Uncle Cyril . . ."

"I know he doesn't . . ."

"You *might* still be chasing up what he said."

Again, Davey missed his chance. He could have told her that all he'd come for was the off-chance of bumping into her – even though he'd still give his eye-teeth to know what the old beggar had meant. Instead, he said, "He's got a pub, hasn't he?"

"Not round *here*."

The other kid cleared his throat.

"You coming in to see Mum?" Claire wanted to know.

"No thanks – just out for a ride. I'm always out this way, training rides."

"Ah."

"You're late from school, aren't you?"

"Orchestra."

"Ah." Again! "What do you play?"

"*The* violin." At which she took the instrument the boy was carrying – carrying for her – and thanked him with one of those smiles.

The boy said, "See you tomorrow" and walked on along the pavement. And if ever Davey wanted to ask someone whether they were engaged to be married, it was right then. But a new pain inside reckoned he knew without asking.

"*This* your bike?"

"No, it's a combine harvester."

Claire widened her eyes at him. "*V* funny," she said. "Well, mine's *not* sleek like this, but I could keep up with you, any day."

"I bet you could."

"What you doing on Saturday?"

Davey wanted to lean the bike against the nearest tree and steady himself. After all this, was she asking him out?

"I'm not doing nothing – anything. Well, I was, but I don't have to . . ."

"No, *don't* change anything for me . . ." She started to go towards her gate.

But, not again – he wasn't going to blow her out again! "There's a circuit race at Crystal Palace I was going in for. But they hold them regular. I've got a racing licence."

"*Have* you? What time?"

"Nine-thirty."

"Right, you *win* your race and we'll go off out Keston way after. Yeah?"

"Yeah, be nice . . ."

"See you here, half eight?"

"Half eight."

"It won't sap your strength before the race?"

"What won't?"

"Coming out here?"

"No way!"

Claire frowned. "Are you all right? You look all *red*."

"No, I'm all right. Been sprinting." But he wasn't all right. Davey Booth was close to having a hot flush. All day on Saturday, after Crystal Palace, he was going to have Cousin Claire to himself! But before he rode off in seventh heaven, Davey had to know one thing.

"That boy . . ." he said. "What instrument does he play? In the orchestra?" He tried to make it sound as if he played something himself.

"Oh, *he's* fabulous," Claire said. "Same as me, violin, but he's the leader. We share the same stand, and the other girls want to *scratch* out my eyes."

"Ah." And Davey wished he'd never asked.

Second fiddle! Wasn't life a send-up!

Chapter Eight

DAVEY WAS up in the air enough, thanks, over the bike chat with his dad. Which was *not* going to be easy, unless he was in one of his move-it-on moods; because John Booth could be mean and sticky, stubborn as a goat going backwards. Or he could be a push-over. Sometimes if you waved your homework at him and said, "Sorted!" he'd want to go through it and make you do a messy page again. Also, he could be right off-hand; say stuff like, "Good lad – bring us in a beer, will you?" It was the job he did as a Transport Manager, one minute on his Motorola hiring and firing, the next going through drivers' logs like a tax inspector.

Still, cycling back, Davey had felt that inch taller on account of Claire. After all, whatever old Nigel Kennedy was to her all the week, Davey wouldn't be second fiddle on Saturday. Enough of a boost to send him in with a skip.

But – crap luck – his dad had to be wearing his tax inspector's hat!

Davey had put his bike in the garage and come in through the back door bursting with his plan – laid it out in the open before he changed his shoes or his mind.

"Decision, folks!" he said. "Davey's come to a decision." This was to his mum in the kitchen, who was brewing up. He went on through to where his dad was watching cricket on Sky. "Dad, got five minutes?" He stood leaning on the table, awkward on the plates of his cycle shoes.

"Can it wait till the end of the innings?"

"Just to tell you I've made my mind up, that's all." But the bad news was, his dad was prepared to take his eye off the match in the middle of a wicket over.

"You've chosen your options?"

"Not yet. That's next year."

"Well, what is it?" Now he pressed the red button and blanked out the screen, faced Davey square. "Come on, lad, spit it out."

Davey took in a deep breath. No way was this going to be an easy ride! He shouldn't have come on so heavy, so *Grandad*, but he'd just wanted to sound certain.

"The bike's wrong. For me." It was out now.

He'd started.

"*Wrong?* What d'you mean, *wrong?* It wasn't wrong yesterday, it wasn't wrong last week, it wasn't wrong when you dragged me round to Bell's house and I bought it for you."

He even remembered the boy's name. No doubt he could quote the numbers on the notes he'd paid with.

"There's nothing wrong *with* it. I don't mean that. No, it's a cracking bike. It's just wrong for what I want ..."

"And what *do* you want?"

Davey's mum had come in now, all ears, family conference. It was the same as when he used to get a roasting over something to do with Grandad; she'd hover. Right now he knew he was as scarlet as those geraniums in their pot. Sweating hot in his cycling gear, he must have looked as if he'd just finished a criterium round London; but this was nothing to do with effort. It was all guilt and frustration.

"I want to specialise in track racing ..."

"So ...? You have been doing." Subject closed. His dad was leaning for the remote to pull the cricket back.

"I want to switch the Wingrave for a decent track bike."

Which had his dad up and switching off the set altogether. "You *what*? After what I paid for it? After ten days? Between haircuts, you want rid of something I paid over the odds to get for you?"

The end of the story, the knock-back. No result. So much for front, spronce, attack-attack-attack! Davey wanted to cry; but he knew how to plead.

"I didn't know then. But now I *do* want to specialise. I'm good at track. They reckon I've got a future at it. I want to be the next Olympic champion."

"And I want to be Queen of the May."

"John!" This from Davey's mum.

"Well, I'm all for ambition, but he's a kid yet. He's too young to go down the one road. Besides, his club's got bikes galore over at Herne Hill. Tell me what's wrong with them." He swung back on Davey. "And what are you going to get about on round the streets? A hoop and a stick?"

Davey walked out of the room. In this mood, there was no winning an argument with the man. He'd said no, and he meant no. He never budged off a no, never, not for anyone, he reckoned it was weak.

Davey went upstairs, peeled off his lycras and grabbed a towel for a shower. He looked down at his unbruised body and his unbroken limbs –

where he'd be taking the beating-up when it came. He looked in the mirror. And how would he ever kiss Claire with no front teeth and stitched lips? Caught between Jarvis and his dad, what would he be good for?

Not that he was going to find out yet – because the next day, miracle of miracles, Jarvis wasn't at school. After a night of twisting and a breakfast of deep breaths, Davey went to school feeling like a crook who's let down the mob. But there was no Jarvis in the yard and no Jarvis swaggering into the tutor room, and after half an hour school started to feel the way school ought to; Miss Briggs losing her hard face, Dan Brewer making a joke and getting a laugh, the relief of no one having to clap Jarvis's farts. It all felt whatever *normal* was.

And soon on, a likely cause of Jarvis's absence put his head round the door. Mr Julien, PE.

"Mr Jarvis?" he asked Miss Briggs.

"Absent," she told him, with one of those looks over her glasses.

"Ah!" said Mr PE. He'd got a result. Mr Jarvis was declining his invitation to a chat. "Pull my wire if he comes in late?"

"Will do."

Which was when Mr Julien's eyes roved the

room and he spotted Davey. "How about this one?"

"David?" Miss Briggs hitched her head at Davey – and he went out of the room to see what the man wanted.

"This here Jarvis ..." he said. He was doing a relaxed lean on the wall, which took some holding, over a broken chair.

"Yeah?"

"Is he givin' you grief?"

Davey shrugged. Was he! But news of it wasn't for Mr PE. What went on between the Booths and the Jarvises wasn't for teachers – stomach muscles, tracksuits or not. Teachers weren't round behind the lavs at dinner time, weren't down the chip shop after school, weren't on the tops of buses where the drivers couldn't see. No teacher had sprung out of a doorway and grabbed Jarvis's handlebars when he was chasing after Davey last night. Their patrols finished when they got in their cars to go home; their flashing blue lights switched off the second they pushed their CDs in. So, no way was Davey going to unwrap the bandages on his Jarvis wounds.

"You won't get nothin' stopped if you don' tell no one about it."

"Nothing *to* stop."

"Is that right?"

"That's right."

"What he done in Assembly was just part of the fun of comin' to school?"

"Wouldn't miss it for nothing."

Mr Julien pushed himself off the wall. "You're south London; you ever heard of Frank Fraser?"

"Who's he play for?"

"One o' the top teams. The Richardsons, big crooks, scared people stupid. But when he got grassed up, he went down for a long, long stretch."

"An' you want me to grass up Jarvis?"

"He won' get stopped if *someone* don't."

Davey stared at the man, narrowed his eyes. Here it was on a plate, it had to be said. Imagine waving Jarvis goodbye, him shut up in one of those white Securicor jobs with the black windows. A result, if you could get it. But, "He's no problem to me," Davey said. And as the bell rang, Mr PE showed his bottom teeth at Davey's lack of bottle, and went to bounce through his day on the sprung gymnasium floor. Some jacks just didn't want to help themselves.

Jarvis took the rest of the week off. But word from the Loyals said he'd only eaten something rotten and was spacing his guts from the school canteen.

He'd be back.

Without the loom of the tyrant, though, there was the chance to think about Saturday – Saturday, all day on his bike with Claire, at Crystal Palace and then out Keston way. Just the two of them, finding out their favourite things, trying on what made each other laugh. Locking their bikes and going for a walk in the woods. Holding hands. Who knew, having a kiss . . .?

A warm sun came in through the classroom window and Davey felt the sweet squeeze in the stomach that he'd had looking at Sam and Louise in Margate; and there wasn't another feeling Davey had ever had which was like it: a honeyed wave to wallow in as he saw Claire's blue eyes, fair hair in bunches, her mouth on the smile, and those long, smooth legs that had straddled Grandad's bike. It made his mouth fill up.

"Hands on the desk, son! What's going on in there?" Dan Brewer rapped on Davey's head, sharp as a bone in a fleshy mouthful.

Davey swallowed. "Nothing."

"I'll buy a piece of that nothing, then! It's put a smile on your kite."

"Yeah?" But Davey tried to keep the smug off his face. It hadn't happened yet – Claire, and Saturday – and the way things were going right

104

now he was taking nothing as read. He could be on a life support up at the A and E by Saturday. He was still a few bad nights off his dreams coming true.

And a quick pull on the brakes was called for – because he mustn't show too much of himself to Dan Brewer this week. The kid hadn't got his racing licence yet, so it wasn't likely he *would* go to Crystal Palace, but you never knew with him, especially if he thought Davey was going. And wasn't he just the sort to edge his wheel between Davey's and Claire's? *A run out Keston – great!* He'd see being there as a challenge. So keep things shtum, Davey told himself – be a solitary man.

"Everything's all a bit tucked up for a couple of weeks," he told Dan, sounding like his dad.

"OK, son, just let your mates know when you're back to normal." And Dan Brewer went off to find another seat.

Crystal Palace park was a regular circuit: not in the athletics stadium, but on the old motor-racing track: *Sport for All* – with Saturday mornings mainly for the youth. Davey was a regular; but this week the ten-lap under-sixteen race would count for winner's points on his licence; and Thames Reach would be picking the borough team for the

London Youth Games, so a good wheel would be expected to make a fair showing today.

That's if broken bones ever let Davey become a good wheel.

But he'd put all that in his back pocket as he'd woken on the Saturday morning. His grandad used to say, "Keep your eye on the feller"; but today was today. Today was Crystal Palace, and Claire, and no one was going to take it off him.

He'd met her outside her house. Auntie Glad had waved from the front door to see them off – only the quickest of flaps back, because where else would Davey be concentrating but on Claire. Without looking as if she'd taken any trouble at all, hell casual, she'd stood there with her bike like an advert for the joys of a life on wheels. No helmet, but a cool baseball cap on the back of her head, a short pink top with a bare strip of belly, and faded raspberry shorts down to somewhere round the knees. Calvin Klein sunglasses, pink ankle socks, new trainers, and a small Nike rucksack.

"Hiya!" Davey couldn't help it but he'd said it to her belly button.

"Am I all right?"

"Sure." *Was* she?!

"For Crystal Palace? They won't *throw* me out without a helmet?"

"Why? You're not racing." Which gave the lie to all his lid talk back in Grandad's shed.

"You never *know*, do you?"

"Tell you what, it's windy up there."

"I've got a top in my Nike."

"Ah." Now Davey had looked at her bike; a Peugeot tourer, nice job. In his own saddle-bag he'd got his trainers and a couple of padlocks for when they went for a walk. No food, but a tenner in his licence wallet.

They'd headed single file off for Crystal Palace, Davey checking in every shop window that she was still there – it wasn't all a dream. And when they'd got to the park, he'd led her through to the circuit with the serious face of someone just daring any whoops or whistles from the Wheelers. No show-ups.

The under-sixteen race was the first. The start and finish was by the terrace of the old long-gone Crystal Palace. A sharp left-hander took you back on yourself for thirty metres or so before a right ran down the hill to a lake at the bottom, where you went around it, and up a hard pull to the top again; before a long left had you racing downhill to the finish. Just under a mile.

It was no doddle, but if you had a bit of what Stan Barrett the trainer called "soupeless" and you'd done your bench presses and squats in the back garden, you had the legs to give it a good go. And did you know you'd raced it when you finished! Which was why Davey had a wet flannel, an under-arm squirt and a spare shirt in his saddle-bag. He didn't want Claire keeping her distance.

And if one race official had to speak to her, they all did – all the old men of the cycle world, clutches of paper and clipboards, important faces and big eyes. "Are you racing?" "What club are you?" "First time here, young lady?" Until she went off to sit in a sunny alcove under the terrace, out of everyone's way.

Davey fished out his licence and signed in. Stan Barrett's wife had set up her table at the rear of their Astra, tailgate in the air, boot for a seat; checking everyone in and dishing out the racing numbers. Davey signed in on the sheet, became rider number eleven, handed over his licence in exchange for his shirt number and two safety pins.

"What tyres are you on, Davey?" Stan Barrett was looking critically at the Wingrave.

"Semi-slicks. Continental Avenues."

"So where's your racing tyres?"

"I'm going out, after."

"An' I'm at a dinner tonight, but I'm not in my bib an' tucker." Stan Barrett was already walking away. *Youth!* You could see it in his long arms and dangling fingers. *Why couldn't they keep their minds on the job?*

The Wingrave had come with two pairs of wheels, one pair with street tyres, the other with racing tyres. Most times Davey would have carried a spanner and made the change before the race, unless – quite rare – he'd come in the car with the bike on the roof. But what would he do with a spare pair of wheels on a ride out with Claire? And, anyway, his street tyres were hybrids, none of those mountain-bike knobbles. He could race on these.

Every other look over to the arches to check on Claire, he wanted to pinch himself that this wasn't all a dream. And there she was, eyes fixed on him, because every time he looked, she waved.

He greeted a couple of club mates and warmed up with a medium-fast lap round the mile. Davey was in his white and blue Reach Wheelers top. Going round with him were Catford Cycling, Anerley BC and the Velo Club de Londres, all the usual turn-out.

"All right?"

"All right?"

Not much more said.

It was always a jolt to the system, coming here

after Herne Hill; to a road circuit with lumps and bumps instead of the smooth of the dedicated velodrome.

The race marshals were taking their places round the course, red flags and whistles.

"Give it some, Davey!"

"Let's have you today!"

He reckoned on about fifteen minutes for the race, once it was under way; then the sixteen to nineteen Juniors would be doing their twenty laps. By which time Davey Booth would be changed and daisy fresh, heading for the country with Claire. Already, out there on the circuit, he was in a little corner of heaven.

He free-wheeled down the final slope to the line, took a quick look that Claire was still under her arch. Which she was, and waving again. What a fan! Riders were being lined up by the Race Commissar, Ted Spencer, king of south-east cycling, pre-war Olympics, all that; shortish, seventies, thick white hair and a tongue on him that could roast the kidneys inside you. If you took a hand off a handlebar and wobbled, he'd burst your tyres with the fire on his voice.

"Come on, let's have you, we ain't got all day!" He checked every rider's number with the care of a miners' overman. "Where's twenty-six?"

"Dunno. Still on a warm-up?"

"He'll warm up for nothing if he ain't quick!" Ted Spencer looked round, shouted over at the clutch of parents and cars. "*Twenty-six!*" He read off the signing-in sheet he'd been given. "Reach Wheelers, Dan Brewer. Where are you?"

Dan Brewer?

Davey Booth pulled his eyes off the tarmac and shot looks all ways. "He hasn't got a licence," he told Ted Spencer.

"I have now, son!" And there was Dan pushing over from the table with his Moser Forma.

"When d'you get that?"

"Came this morning. Stuck my picture on, and here I am!"

"Great!" *Cobblers!* more like.

"Come on, lad, get in there next to Booth." Ted Spencer was flapping his papers and looking over at the lap marshal. "Right, you all ready?"

No one answered, which meant they were.

"Go on, then, get off with you." Which was all there was to a circuit start.

With a cracking of gears the first two lines got away; followed by a second batch of slower wheels, girls in both batches; about thirty riders overall.

But Davey wasn't hanging about. Straight off,

he stood out of the saddle and went for the first bend with his legs blurring in gear twenty-three, and Dan with him like a man who'd been racing all his life.

"Should have clocked your face! Seeing me! Bit of a turn-up, eh?"

Davey grunted. He could say that again! But Brewer suddenly showing up was a turn upside down more like. And forget the race, it was a turn upside down of Davey's day.

Chapter Nine

"GOOD EH? Me getting my licence?"
"Brilliant!"

Starting in the middle of the front row, they hadn't hit the first bend in the front. Davey flicked the bike up a gear with his thumb and went after the leaders who had – Johnnie Butcher of Reach and Sylvie Lennard of Astra. Twenty metres of flat led to the right-hander down the fast drop to the lake. Half a metre back, Dan Brewer with him all the way, he moved up another gear for the push downhill; a tight pack, cracking up their sprockets at speed, heads down for least drag as they all went racing for the bend at the bottom. And the same order as it came at them, flicks on brakes, free-wheeling, leaning into the bottom straight. And Dan Brewer still with breath for a word.

"See that girl waving at you?"
"What girl?"
"Drop dead gorgeous!"

No reply – anyhow, Davey was saving his breath for the pull. A left at the end of the straight, down two gears, and out of the saddle, hands high on the bars, up the long slope to the top: the place to attack the two in front.

And Dan Brewer still with him, matching him. He was fit, was Dan – a quick look showed the man he was getting to be. Broad shoulders, strong arms; and meaty ... And eyes everywhere, he'd clocked Claire, hadn't he? What a snarl-up!

A long left bend at the top of the rise and the pack whirred down to the start, Davey on the right picking up half a metre on Sylvie Lennard. And still not losing Dan Brewer. Past the chat of officials at the start, the leading riders' numbers taken for the lap records.

"There! Under that arch."

Davey looked over. Claire was waving again.

"Go *on*, Davey!"

"See?"

"Not me. Some other kid."

And into the first bend for the second time. What a slap! Because the race wasn't top any more, not till he could come up with some answer to Dan Brewer. Dan had ridden over here on his own – always did – was racing on street tyres the same as Davey, meaning he was out for the day, he'd be in for the crack, stringing along. No way would Dan think three was a crowd; he'd think the ride was for the exercise.

Head down at the fast lake drop and Davey made another move up on Sylvie Lennard; reckoned if he braked late when she free-wheeled into the bottom bend, he could take her on the outside and pump it along the straight.

Except for Dan Brewer sitting there on his outside – leaving no room for the manoeuvre: neck and neck and racing more like a yellow jersey than some kid whose licence hadn't dried. And *still* with breath for a word.

"Come for a run, after?"

Davey's answer was a spurt. No way! But he'd used up all his grandad excuses; he wouldn't have come racing this morning if he'd been as tucked up as he'd pretended. And after a club run he and Dan always went for a McDonald's, or a Coke in Gerry Gelato's ...

Out of the saddle again, up the long pull for the second time, and Davey losing road to get himself on the left of the pack, where Claire wouldn't get a clear bead on him as he passed the start; wanting Dan to forget her. Which lost him concentration, and speed. So this time it wasn't Claire who yelled at him as he crossed the line.

"Come on, Davey Booth! Where's your *push*?!" Stan Barrett was hopping.

Davey put his head down and went for the first bend again. Where *was* his push? What was he here for? He needn't have come at all if he wasn't here for the race, he could have just met up with Claire and gone out to Keston from the off. And he wanted in to the London Youth Games. So he'd got to put in a good time – and then be slick as soap after it, or else he might just as well pull up with a wobbly wheel and get off before the end.

No – the order was, ride a good race, and then lose Dan. And a tall order. Davey didn't mind being bested by Johnnie Butcher – Johnnie was older and built different, ranked higher – Stan Barrett wouldn't expect him to be beating Johnnie for a season or two. But he'd expect him to do Sylvie Lennard, *and* in style. So, in the wild hope there'd be a life after Jarvis, Davey had got to show everyone the pro he was going to be. *Plus*, know what to do about gooseberry Dan Brewer.

But first he had to see him off on the circuit. And Davey hadn't been doing this for a few months without picking up a few tricks. He knew how to wobble a front wheel when a rival was close and a marshal wasn't looking – shout "Sorry!" because anyone could lose it on a rough road. He knew when to strain himself changing up a gear quick after a bend, stand out of the saddle like uphill and gain a metre while the others were thinking about it. He knew when to shoot on into a bend and brake suddenly, getting a metre in front – and not to do it next time round when he was expected to, so his rival said hello to the verge.

Today, he pulled all these stunts – and by lap six he was second to Johnnie Butcher, Sylvie Lennard on his back wheel now, and Dan Brewer fourth or fifth somewhere.

He'd stopped looking and worrying whether Claire was waving – it was everything for the race. What came after, came after.

"That's better, son – now go for Johnnie!" Stan Barrett had changed the pipes in his throat to something more melodious.

And Davey did – although he was never going to crack him. But as the bell went for the last lap, his front wheel was only two inches from Johnnie's back. Down the drop, round the lake, out of the saddle on the last slope and giving it everything in a gear higher than he should, to come out of it into the last run-in with his head thrown forward in the Superman position.

Shouts and cheers for a cracking finish! Half a bike in it, a shock for Johnnie Butcher. And flashing top speed past the line, everyone went on another quarter-mile, slowing and unwinding, getting their breathing to something near normal. Johnnie waved victory and went on; Sylvie Lennard waved third and went on; Dan Brewer and a small pack kept their heads down and went on, round the first bend and on down the slope towards the lake.

But Davey Booth braked sudden and hard, left half a tyre on the tarmac in a black exclamation and raced over the grass to a jumping Claire, shouted at her.

"Come on! We go!"

And they went. No stopping for reasons, no having to know the ins and outs of what he was up to, Claire went. A cracker, an oppo – it ran in the family.

Until they were out of the park and pedalling up to the roundabout. "Who *are* we getting away from?"

"A mate of mine. He'll want in on our day."

"Will he? And you reckon I'm *too* special for that?"

"Tons. Miles."

Davey scraped a left round the first street turning: off the main road in case Dan Brewer came after: then left, then a right, lost them both in the backstreets where only a tracking device would have found them. They stopped.

"An' that's lost us *all*," Claire said. "What road's this?"

"Still Crystal Palace." Davey looked up at the street name. "Farquhar."

She gave him a look.

Farquhar Road? Davey looked at it again. Didn't that ring a bell? He knew of a Farquhar Road. You didn't forget a name like "Farquhar".

Claire was ready for pushing off.

"Hang on!"

"What to?"

"You know who used to live in this street?"

"Couldn't *begin* to guess."

"Louise. Our nan. Grandad's wife. Sam Butler's girlfriend, when they met." He gabbled out to Claire about the photo he'd found with the address on the back.

"What number?"

"One-two-eight. Let's find it and sell them a sign to put up."

"*Not!* I don't want to cruise round these old streets. I want to get out to Keston." And she put the shock of a cool hand on his hot arm, lost them both their balances, and ran a chain print of bike oil across the back of her leg.

"Oh, *lovely*!" Claire looked over her shoulder down at her calf. A perfect print. You could almost see the rivets. Davey bent to look, but went red being down there so close to her skin and didn't hang about.

"You want to use powder graphite."

"To get it off?"

"Instead of oil. Next time."

"Cheers! *Next* time I won't grab you!"

"Sorry." Davey looked about him. Not a good start! They could have mended a puncture, adjusted her forks, lowered her saddle – but they couldn't vanish a black track of Number One Oil.

"I'll have to go home. I *can't* parade round Keston like this."

No, not back to Auntie Glad! Davey thought. But over the road, on the next corner, there was a small shop.

"Let's have a look in there. They might have a bottle of white spirit ..."

But Claire was already scooting to it, leaning her bike on a lamppost and pushing in through the bleep of the door. Davey locked their bikes and followed.

There was an old woman serving, wispy hair done up on top and a Crystal Palace football shirt. The shop was empty, apart from a girl unpacking a case of baked beans. Claire went to the counter, turned round, showed the back of her leg to the shopkeeper.

"Have you got a small pack of tissues and something for this? Please."

"Come off your bike, love?" Apart from the football top, the old woman looked as if she'd been behind that counter for sixty years.

"Sort of."

The old woman laughed, high and thin. "It was always happening to me. Bike chains, skate wheels comin' off. Right tomboy, I was. Rode my bike down the stairs one time, went clear through the glass of the front door."

"Why?"

"'Cos the door weren't open."

"No, why ride down the stairs?"

The old woman pulled a face. "Didn't have a telly in them days. Made our own amusement." She laughed again – one of those old London characters you didn't get in Safeways. "Come on, love, you don't want to spend out on that. Nice young feller waiting ..." Although she hadn't looked up. "Doreen – take this young lady out the back and get a rag to this leg, an' a spot of stuff from under the sink."

Doreen left unpacking her baked beans, lifted

the counter flap for Claire and led her through to the back.

"Thanks *ever* so much."

"'s all right. Bli', can't have your day out done in by a blessed bicycle chain."

Davey came over to thank the old woman again. But he hadn't opened his mouth when she winked at him. "Nice little thing. Pretty. I like to see it." Which she didn't explain, but sent Davey red again.

And he hadn't meant to say anything other than "Ta", but covering his confusion he suddenly heard himself getting in deeper.

"Have you been here long?"

"Since six a'smorning."

"No, like *years*."

"I'll say years. I was born upstairs, right above where I'm standing here."

"Ah."

"My grandfather's, this was, then my father's, then my brother's and mine. But 'e went down on the *Rodney*, thanks to 'itler."

"I was wondering if you knew my nan. She lived down this road."

"Name of . . .?"

"Louise Freeman, she'd be then."

And it was as if he'd said *Put 'em up! Open that*

122

till! Don't move or you get it! The old woman stepped back, stiff as a corpse, face white to match. Her soft old eyes turned to ball bearings.

"Your grandmother, was she? Well, I tell you, boy, don't come all 'Louise Freeman' round here!" Her voice wasn't high any more, it was more like Stan Barrett on a growl.

"Why? What's up with her?"

The old woman shouted through into the back. "You done in there, Doreen? Come on, don't give it all day! I need you in the shop!"

Davey was halfway to the door. He'd wait for Claire outside before the old girl had a heart attack.

"You want to do everyone a favour, boy?"

Davey faced her. Deep breath.

"Go an' put a gallon of arsenic in the beer over the Kentish Arms. From the decent folk of Far-quhar Road."

A customer came in, an old man. She told him, too. "I'm just telling this boy here he can go an' put arsenic in the beer over the Kentish."

"Never use it," the old man said. "Never have." And he turned to Davey, white stubble, hair out of every crack, old age grown all over his face. "*Wouldn't!*" he told him, like an oath. "Us older ones'd sooner go dry than drink in there."

123

Davey went outside and unlocked the bikes. He felt as if he'd been rollicked at school by some bad-tempered teacher, or sworn at by a swinging drunk.

Claire followed out, red leg where the oil had been; and a straight face to match Davey's.

"What's up with her? She changed like Jekyll and Hyde, *couldn't* get me out quick enough."

Davey shrugged. "I dunno." And he didn't. He pushed off, led the way down the road, no eyes bothering for Dan Brewer any more.

What *was* all this about his grandad's family? What was this ghost of the past he felt forever wraithing around him, this *something* he kept touching but couldn't get a grip on?

Chapter Ten

IT WAS like the shred of foil in the mouth that comes from round a fruit pastille; Davey's sweet day had taken a tinny taste. The woman in that shop had just churned up the Uncle Cyril turmoil and the twist in the gut from Grandad's old girlfriend. What *was* all that about? Davey would be forever upset till he knew; and being out on his own with the lively Claire suddenly wasn't the treat he'd been living for.

Head down, he led the way through the streets of Crystal Palace; and only at a set of lights where Claire swerved in and stalled a bus did he find out where he was going.

"Oi! Number eleven! Rest of the pack went the other way!" The bus driver should have been on *Jokers Wild*.

Number eleven! Davey felt round his waist; he'd still got his racing number on. In the sprint to get away from Dan Brewer he hadn't returned his number – and he hadn't claimed his licence back.

But Claire was going on about directions. "This is *not* the way to Keston!"

"Isn't it?"

"It is *not*. Are you lost without men waving red flags?"

"Sorry – you want to go in front?"

"You're taking us out Farningham way ..."

"Am I?"

"What's out there?"

The lights changed and Claire got a toot. But along the next stretch, wider and with more space, she came up on his inside again. And he told her.

"What's out there is Eynsford. You ever been to Eynsford?"

She hadn't.

"Want to?"

"I'm out with *you*; I'll go where you go."

He smiled, a bit of the pastille coming back. "That's all right, then. I'll take you to Eynsford."

Eynsford. The river crossing where the car had got stuck and he and Grandad had met the ex Old Bill in the pub; the place where Hard Stew had kissed Claire in the dream. Now he was taking her there for real. But he couldn't say why. Was it to put paid to a rotten nightmare, to see off at least *one* of his ghosts?

One thing, Eynsford didn't change: because there was nothing at Eynsford that *could* change, except the depth of the water. The river still ran through, the grassy bank was still grassy and flat, the shaggy cattle still grazed on the far side, and the old stone bridge still had its two arches leading through into the darkness. It was all the same as Davey remembered it.

Except, there was no Grandad any more, lounging like a picnicker on the grass; and, please God, no Stuart Jarvis under that bridge.

"*This* is nice! Why haven't I been here before?"

You could search Davey. They were sitting cross-legged on the bank, he'd taken off his racing numbers, was like any other Saturday tourist and was about to go over to the café by the bridge and get them a roll and a Coke.

"Came here with Grandad. We pushed someone out who'd driven through and wet his plugs."

"*Big* mistake. Wetting your plugs."

She was always on the up, Claire; when you were serious, she was light; if you were light, she was deep.

And he'd said it before he thought about it. Forget the roll and Coke for a bit.

"Fancy a paddle?"

"In the water?"

"That's where you paddle."

"Is it wet?"

"Could be."

"Lovely! Cool down my hot feet." And, actions to words, it was off with her trainers and her socks.

Davey fumbled with his. A simple thing, taking off their shoes and socks. So why had he gone red again? Was it because her bare feet were gorgeous feet, no lumps or bumps like his mum's, and tipped in coral nail polish?

"*Come* on then. And no splashing or pushing – I've only got what I'm standing up in."

Which wasn't a lot. Davey felt the need to splash his face and neck with cold water; but instead he took the hand she was holding out to him, and trying not to show the pain of the odd sharp stone and the clumpy grass, he went with her into the water.

It was cool and balmy, both at once. He could see how washing your hot feet in a dusty country had to have a great feel. The river was low and running slowly, and there were others mucking about at its edge: a few kids throwing stones for the plop of it; a woman sitting letting the water suck at her toes, her husband next to her and – big kid himself – having to kick and splash.

But the river bed was mud and slip, and Claire's hand in Davey's was gripping tight. If one went, they both went; and somehow, in that moment of happiness, whooping and laughing, they were both up for risking that.

"*Didn't* bring a towel!"

"No."

"Think what my mum would have said if I had! She'd have only thought we were going skinny dipping!"

"As if ..." Oh, God, the thought of that! Now it wasn't just the danger of a red face Davey was up against! Suddenly, there in the middle of the River Darent, he felt the urgent need to start saying a few difficult multiplications. "Come on!" Keeping going, he led the way to the middle of the ford, past the first of the arches under the bridge.

"Where does that go?"

"Under the bridge ..."

"I can see *that*, Brainbox. Where?"

"Downstream." To where Jarvis had kissed Claire in the dream.

"Yes, *downstream*! But what's through there?"

Davey peered under. "A field, a reccy sort of place; and Eynsford Castle."

"Castles, even!" Now she was leading him, under the arch. It was like that weird brain thing where you've been there before. Through they went, where it was dark, and out at the other side where the river was dappled by the shadowing trees.

"Secret! It's like your own *world* through here. Like Alice in Wonderland. Only with no one about to see you ..."

She turned to him, and just as if it were written in a script, neither of them being the first, neither of them being the second, they kissed. He stared seriously into her eyes, she stared seriously into his. His arms went round her waist, hers went round his neck, and their mouths met. And though Davey had only ever kissed before in hot rushed games of chase, missing the mark and with the girl's hair always in the way, he kissed Claire as if he'd been doing it all his life. Their tongues met and made their own sweet talk while up to his knees the water boiled.

Till breath ran out. "An' you've been my cousin all the time!" he said.

"Except, you didn't want to know in your grandad's shed."

"I did – but I was all up in the air."

"You haven't exactly got your feet on the ground right now!"

"I have – it's ground under water, isn't it?"

And they stared at each other, were about to go for it again, when one of the kids who'd been throwing stones came following under the arch. Kids had to follow, didn't they? This one stopped, stood and watched them, as if they were a tourist attraction: next best to a car getting its plugs wet. So Davey filled the moment with talk, still holding her.

"What would old Uncle Cyril say if he came sculling through here right now?"

"'Good luck!' I reckon. He's not such an old fuddy..."

"I s'ppose you can't be, running a pub."

"*And* he's always there, serving."

The kid was still watching.

"So, where is it, his pub?" As if they'd come under here for a chat.

"Not far from where we were..."

"Crystal Palace?"

"That way. Different part."

The water was suddenly starting to run cold.

"What's it called?"

Claire looked at the kid too. "Had your eyeful?" she asked him.

The kid turned and paddled back the way he'd come. Claire looked serious at Davey again, dropped her voice to a murmur as they came together for their second kiss. "'The Kentish Arms'," she said, into his mouth.

And this time the taste of it was tin foil. But how was it he'd known that was the answer she was going to give him? The pub the old woman wanted poisoned.

The shadows of the tall trees had crossed the road when Davey said goodbye to Claire at her gate. They'd had a good long day round the lanes and in the gateways of Kent, and he only hoped she hadn't noticed how different his inside had been working to his outside; hoped his voice hadn't sounded as down in the throat to her as it had to him. He wanted to think he'd been a laugh, good company, that she hadn't cottoned on how his heart hadn't been in the rest of the day, after that second kiss.

Now it was time to go their own ways; now was when he found out where he stood.

"See you, then," he said.

She nodded.

"One night, if you're not too busy with your violin . . ."

"We're *always* busy with our violins . . ."

We! That old lemon squeeze of jealousy. Her and Nigel Kennedy sharing the same sheet of music.

"But half term's coming," he said. "Is yours the same as mine?"

It was, the Whit week. The week after next.

"Bank Holiday Monday. What if we go out for a run again, like today?"

"Could do. Talk to you on the phone, eh?" And she went in. No kiss goodbye, not even a peck. It was like the night they'd first met here in the road; Davey left with that feeling of wanting to go at a punchball, or shout some curdle loud enough to be heard over the whole of south London.

He cycled home, the direct route, no longer on the look-out for anyone, his head a mix of sweet memory, tinny taste, jealousy and bewilderment: the day out with Claire, what she'd said, what he'd said, and the way she'd left things all up in the air: gone indoors quicker than a rabbit down a hole. So was she ashamed afterwards about the kiss? Or did she have to sort out how she felt, between him and her violin? Had he just had the old cold goodbye; and she'd never be in if he phoned? Had he pushed his luck? Because as far as he could see they'd done that kiss *together*.

More like, Davey Booth just wasn't much fun. Perhaps he was boring as hell up against the other blokes Claire knew...

But it wasn't how Claire felt he should have

been worried about. And he shouldn't have let the faffing of his heart make him careless.

Because Stuart Jarvis hadn't gone away. As Davey cycled past the common ravine, half a kilometre from home, out of nowhere he was hemmed in like the Tour de France. A whole pack of bikes, Stuart Jarvis and the Loyals, on everything from Raleighs to Rourkes. They came clattering him and sent him scraping along the kerb; off his bike, them off theirs in a bundle of bodies which had him on to the common and pinned by the shoulders to the prickly grass.

"Boove!"

"Get off! What?" They'd got him down, but where were the punches and kicks? Anyone passing would think it was no more than a spotties' romp, just a big kid sitting on another kid's stomach.

"That bike, son! You're still ridin' the 'kin thing. You riding round to show me contempt?"

"'Course not . . ."

"'e don't want *contempt*, Booth! 'e wants *respect*," spat a Loyal called Squid.

"Shut up, Squid, I do the mouthin'." And Squid got what Davey hadn't yet, a push in the face.

Davey tried a heave and a wriggle, token, because Jarvis pushed his shoulders down, hard. So, what was he up to? Was it now – a beating-in and a steal of the Wingrave, like he'd threatened?

"*I'll* tell you wha' I want . . ."

Even as Davey stared into Jarvis's flecky mouth he saw his dad down at the nick bringing charges before you could say "Accident and Emergency".

". . . I want on that bike legitimate. You're *sellin'* it to me, son, wi' no come-backs. Because what Jarvis wants, Jarvis gets. Don' he?"

His Loyals all nodded and tried to look like pirates.

"So, it's end of 'alf term. Or what 'appens won' look like it was down to me or nothin', but I tell you, it won' do your 'elf no good. No 'kin good at all!"

"Yeah . . .!" the Loyals growled.

And Jarvis suddenly got up, just one quick kick as he walked back to get his bike off the pile – swaggering, swinging, that serious, open mouth and Herod eyes. Mr Respect. Al Capone. The Frank Fraser Mr PE had been on about.

Davey got up himself, came away from the top of the ravine. And as if some silent sign had been given, a shoal of piranhas turning like one, the Loyals rounded on him and shoved him hard to catch him off balance and send him rolling down the steep slope, bruising and grazing on the pebble and flint.

When he came to the road again, his bike was still there. Miracle, not a scratch on it, tyres still up, all its bits and pieces untouched. He was no fool, then, Jarvis. He was well on the way to running the streets of south London – into drugs and filth and heists, the way someone always has to be; and someone who didn't intend to get nicked for it. And there were no two ways about it, this was nothing to do with Davey's hand-built Wingrave. This was all about that thing called power.

He'd come off his bike, hadn't he? It happened in races. It happened all the time in the Tour de France – and his mum and dad bought it just as they'd bought the bruising before Grandad had died. The fact that the bike had escaped without a mark wasn't noticed. But what the hell was Davey going to do about Jarvis?

Meanwhile, there he stood having Savlon dabbed and smeared by his mum.

"You had a nice day out with Claire, then?"

"Yeah." So Auntie Glad had phoned.

"Go far?"

"Only Eynsford way . . ."

"It's nice out there."

"Had a good chat." Davey was facing the

picture of his nan, Louise – the portrait on the wall. A sweet face, a lovely lady, never as pretty as Claire, of course ... "She told me about Uncle Cyril's pub ..."

"Oh, yes?" This was Davey's dad, who'd pricked up like a dog hearing the word *walk*.

"The Kentish Arms is it?"

Now his dad was away from the drivers' logs he'd been checking at the table. "He's had it for years ..."

"Ouch!" Davey jumped as his mum slapped his leg, finished.

"You'll live."

Would he?

There was a long moment. Davey's dad half dropped his eyes to his drivers' logs again, but Davey had got up enough speed not to want to put on the brakes.

"Good pub, is it?"

"Dunno. Never been in there myself. Not the nicest corner of London. You couldn't trust your car to still be there when you came out."

"Anyway, we're not ones for pubs, are we, John?" Davey's mum was suddenly making a career out of emptying a cold teapot into the sink.

And that was the end of that. They were definitely avoiding the issue. Which gave Davey nothing else to do but take himself upstairs to look at his wounds – with a long stare into the mirror and a churn again at the thought of what Jarvis would do to him next time. Only, he'd struck now, hadn't he? He'd gone that bit further and shown himself out with detail. Things had to be the way he wanted them. So what would the big one be – what waited for Davey when Jarvis ran out of patience and was pushed to prove his power? Because there was no way out for Davey, except telling his dad or Mr PE – and he had no proof to back anything up.

It put Davey's ups and downs with Claire well into the background. And it sapped at his need to find out anything about Louise from Farquhar Road, and Uncle Cyril's Kentish Arms, and the meaning of those hell remarks about his grandad. Whatever the name of that ghost haunting him, he'd got the name of his own devil scratched into him right now – Hard Stuart Jarvis.

Chapter Eleven

GRANDAD HAD always liked a game of draughts; and straight off he'd say, "Stripe me, the lap o' luxury, got all the pieces ..." Always, never failed. Meaning, whenever he'd played in some army barracks or wherever, they'd had to make up the numbers with bottle tops. And the other dead cert was, when Davey wanted time to think out a move, he'd always come out with, "Time to think, boy? You c'n get too much of that!"

Well, time to think was what Davey needed right now, and plenty of it – time to work out his next move with Jarvis. He'd got next week at school, then it was half term; by the end of which Jarvis wanted on the Wingrave, or he'd end up dead meat. And on his own bike or a club bike, he'd never set Herne Hill alight with two legs in plaster.

That Saturday night, he lay hot on his bed in a

pair of shorts and stared up at the ceiling. His ceiling paper swirled in a complicated pattern, imaginary tracks he often rode round in his head; the long circuit, and the sprint circuit, or the *Tour de Chambre* with its tough alpine section over the wardrobe. And the same way that Claire and Nigel Kennedy no doubt played their fingers up and down imaginary fiddle strings, he flicked finger and thumb on his Ergo gears.

So he lay there going round and round, finger and thumb, finger and thumb, Jarvis, Jarvis, Jarvis – trying to come up with an answer.

He went over everything that had happened about the bike; the advert, the buying, the shock of finding out about Jarvis being in for it; the threats. And the downer of his failed attempt to get his dad onside over the track bike answer. *He* was the alpine section, his dad, he was the hard pull. No way was he young like Grandad, John Booth was *old*, and a real belt and braces man. Everything had to be apple pie – tax all paid up and the cat insured . . .

Which was negative, negative, negative, and in all his depressed staring Davey must have dropped off, because the chill of no bed covers suddenly shivered him to find the light gone, and the circuits on the ceiling disappeared.

He sat up, took a look at Grandad's watch, started to sort himself for the night; when, strewth! it hit him. All those thoughts, awake and then asleep, he'd had the time and some sort of plan was coming . . .

He shook his head to shake it loose if it wasn't going to hold.

"Known facts. Always go on your known facts." That was Grandad whenever something was being sorted. "Eleven times out of ten it's all there, bosh! Smack in front of you." And it had been! "The easy way, mate. An' remember, no mug expects the expected . . ."

He got up, walked round and round the room. So, was he "out of the saddle" and pedalling the Alpe d'Huez like a Pantani? Was it going to hold? Davey went over the simplicity of it and reckoned it could, because he'd got all the pieces in place.

He'd got Jarvis needing to show off his power and get given respect; he'd got Uncle Cyril's pub sitting where you couldn't leave your car and find it later; he'd got the hand-built Wingrave; and he'd got his dad's tax inspector's approach to everything.

It *was* all there! He wanted to clap his hands, punch the air. Simple! Now all he had to work out was the strategy; and that was simple, too, that was the bit no one would expect – the expected.

It was brilliant! Davey jumped back on his bed and cycled in the air at the scam of it. It was all there – only the fine details to be worked out. And wouldn't an up-front girl like Claire approve, if only he could tell her?

Claire. Who else, the Saturday night of his first serious kiss? He had to come back to her. You couldn't just nod off with the taste of that kiss still in your mouth.

But, here came the old doubts again! Solve one problem, Davey Booth, and there's always another to take its place.

How serious had it been for her? Would she have kissed him like that if she hadn't wanted to? She wasn't the sort who went round kissing *anyone* like that, was she? He had this great feeling of respect for her that said she wasn't anyone's idea of an easy goer. But she *had* rushed indoors as if she'd been on the end of a bungey rope; he'd had no sweet goodbye to take home with him.

Up to the kiss, fine, give or take the old woman in the shop: but after finding out the name of the pub, hadn't Davey lost his bounce? No question – he'd blown it himself in a big way by being so quiet all round. Claire probably had tons more fun with Nigel Kennedy, sitting at their music stand;

her turning his music or him turning hers; crossing their bows in the difficult bits.

On the other hand, *vicci verci*, as Grandad would have said, "You're not out the running till they've taken your legs off." Which was true. How many times had Davey thought he hadn't got enough blow for five more miles when he found some, under pressure? How often had his best lap time been faster than he'd reckoned? Enough! Well, he'd see how things were when he phoned her.

Meanwhile, who was talking sleep? He'd got plenty to keep him awake tonight, wriggling round the bed. Kisses. Threats. Bruises. Scams. And wishes: which brought him back to kisses again.

Well, you had to have hope, didn't you?

Back on Planet Earth, it was the last week before half term – school on the Monday, and two people for Davey to face out. Jarvis – although he'd probably done his pieces for a couple of days – and Dan Brewer, who was a problem of a different sort.

And Davey deserved it when Dan turned that face on him that he kept for nerds.

"Smashin' mate to have, you are, Booth!"

"How do you mean?"

"Oh, don't you know, son? Don't you really know – prefer it in writing, would you, easy little words like g-e-t l-o-s-t?"

"Come *on*!"

"Yeah, come on! So Booth had a girl with him! Couldn't *say*, could you? Couldn't give a mate the *sense* to leave you alone for your little outing. No – let's shoot off out of it while Brewer's not looking! Let's leave Brewer feeling like Tuesday's chips!"

"*Dan!*"

"*Brewer.*" And Brewer didn't want to listen to any explanation. Which probably served, because Davey hadn't got one. Dan was right, he'd treated him like dirt – and it would never have been easy telling him he *wouldn't* have had the sense to back off ... So Davey left it, and sat in a spare seat in his sets, before Dan Brewer did.

Definite grief – but on the Jarvis front Mr 'PE' Julien turned out true to form. That Monday morning he made sure Hard Stew found out his memory could span a week. Ten minutes after Jarvis had walked in, into the tutor room came Mr Julien again. It had to have been arranged, because he didn't dance any polite words round Miss Briggs, he just put his head and one arm round the door and crooked his finger at the one he wanted.

"You! Gymnasium A."

"Who?"

"*You!*"

And Jarvis went, after that hold-your-breath moment while everyone wondered whether he would or not. But Jarvis didn't let it weigh, he got up and walked to the door with just a smirk over his shoulder at Squid; his look of contempt for Mr Julien as loud a racist statement as if he'd shouted something.

What happened no one knew: there wasn't a class in the gym during Registration. Whether Jarvis just got the rough end of Julien's tongue, or whether he had to do circuits, Jarvis wasn't going to tell. He came back with nearly the same smirk he'd gone out with. But he stayed clear of Davey in public.

Till the Wednesday – when he let Davey know he was no way off the hook; his Loyals there to hear it all, that being the way power and respect get kept; all standing like bouncers at the door of Jarvis's club – the yard lavatories.

" 'ow's your legs, Boove? Still 'olding you up?"

"They're all right. How's yours?"

"Waitin' to get on that bike . . ."

"Come on, you're not really into bikes, Jarvis . . ."

"No? You think you're the only one, then, do you?"

"No, but—"

"Listen, I'm on that bike, son." He came close with his threat of a face. "It's mine by rights. I 'ad that bike till your ol' man went over the odds for it."

Which was true. And Davey didn't have to rile Jarvis too much, either; there were too many hard basins and stinking lavatory pans around for getting clever with him.

"I'll be out an' about next week, son – which is the end o' your length of rope. So do yourself a bit o' good. I got the dosh – it's all le-git – you bring the bike an' we do the business."

Davey stared into the cold slits of Jarvis's eyes. "Told you I'd do my best."

"An' it 'ad better be best *enough*, 'adn't it?" And with a nod for them to allow anyone in who wanted, Jarvis went over to the Loyals at the door, waiting while they stood aside to let him through.

No, Jarvis hadn't gone away – and he wasn't *going* to go away. Mr PE hadn't solved anything permanent with his gymnasium stunt. Because Davey knew that no one did anything effective about the Jarvises of this world, unless they'd got enough on them to put them out of everyone's way. Davey's problem was still going to have to be solved his way.

He could tell straight off by the numbers on the cars. Car numbers were a few years adrift themselves round Thames Reach; but the stuff parked up in the streets near the Kentish Arms were years older than most of all that. Oil patches stuck to his bike tyres, and old black sacks spilled their guts round gate openings. Once, there had been shops – but most of them were closed up now with dirty nets across the windows, the signs above them flaking like dead skin. Kids played on the pavements, all snot and dummies, the poor of the blacks, whites and mixed races who lived round there making their fun in the tip of a world they'd been dragged into: and what he wanted to see – ones and twos of the gobbing, head-down local youth who'd have the lollies off toddlers as soon as look at them.

And there, lording it above the streets of squat houses, stood the Kentish Arms, a big corner pub, three storeys of it and four-square as a castle; brown paintwork, cream plaster; with *Hotel* still engraved in the glass of one of the doors.

Davey cycled past, didn't want to be seen sussing the area by Uncle Cyril. Like someone hell bent on cycling on through who suddenly changed his mind, he swerved a left past the Kentish Arms into Gibraltar Road, where he nearly ran smack into a skip of old masonry outside a scaffolded repair job.

Well, he could have used that now, he reckoned. Except, it was no good tonight; where would he have been, for telling his dad? In the pub seeing Uncle Cyril on his own, having a shandy on the off-chance? No way – and that was the weak part of his plan; he'd seen that as soon as he'd started on the detail; he needed a reason, such as taking a message from his mum, or being with Claire, who'd popped in to see her grandad. And he needed a witness, not just his word for things. He needed a cover.

But one thing was for certain. *This* was the place to get him off the hook ...

And now Davey could make the phone call he'd been putting off, now he could do the double deal. He could see how he stood with Claire, and he could set up the Wingrave scam.

Heart going, his finger trembling on the buttons, of course he had to get Auntie Glad first. He would, wouldn't he? "Who's speaking? ... Davey. Ah. Hold the line, I'll see if Claire's in." More like,

I'll see if Claire wants to speak to you . . .

"Hiya."

"Is that Claire?"

"*Does* my dad say 'hiya'?"

That voice, the way she put the weight on certain words. That wriggle in his gut. "How you doing?"

"All right. *How* are you?"

"OK."

"Feet dry yet?"

Which was code for the kiss. Twist and shout! "Still a bit damp."

"Mine, too."

A bigger wriggle. Blow out his doubts, here he was talking to the Claire he wanted to hear.

"I was wondering, like I said, half term – how about a ride out . . . ?"

"Yeah – *if* you like . . . Know any more good places?"

"Must be millions."

"Then you get your little Michelin out. Come over here first?"

"OK."

Eureka! And if only he could have left it there; up in his seventh heaven. But there was no way he could blow out Jarvis. Now for the hard bit, the crunch. "Whatever . . . on the way . . . could we go out past Uncle Cyril's pub?"

There was a long wait. "Sorry, I was shaking the phone. *Didn't* hear straight."

"I said—"

"I *thought* you said, go out past Uncle Cyril's pub . . ."

"I did. It's a message I've got, from my mum . . ." It was the best he could come up with.

No response.

"Monday? Tuesday?" he prompted.

"Tuesday. Ten o'clock?"

"Ten o'clock, your place."

Another silence. Davey wanted to say something cheeky, go back to the kiss, talk wet feet; but the twist and shout was gone. Because when two and two were put together, the hell of it was that Tuesday wasn't going to be their lovely day out at all. Tuesday was going to be a mess – the straight shout of it being, he wasn't planning a treat at all, he was planning a cowardly get-out from Jarvis's threats.

"You still *there*?"

He was. "See you Tuesday, then."

"See you Tuesday . . ." Which she sang, operatically. And what he wouldn't have given to sing something himself. But it would only have come out flat, because what he was into was conning Claire.

Conning the girl he reckoned he loved.

Chapter Twelve

WHAT DAVEY had in his hand was a picture of people in love; and he looked at it today for the same reason he looked at it every day – to keep him going in all this grief. He'd gone to his shelf and filleted out the old Margate photograph, his grandad and Louise on the day they'd met up. A sort of good-luck charm. But today it was no quick fix; he sat on his bed and stared at it and stared at it till the people in the picture shimmered and fidgeted; he stared it out of focus and into a sort of life. And he pictured the next move they'd made – some of them looking at the sea and the arcades, but Sam and Louise into each other all day. He'd be like that with Claire at a family 'do', a hall full of family but only the two of them there for real.

Then the blokes probably all went in Dreamland and rode the rides, shot the rifles, saw Thanet and the estuary from the top of the Big Wheel – Louise wanting to tag along, but the other girl not, the party pooper; so Sam and his girl would have split and met later at the kiosk to pick up the picture, where she wrote her name on his print, and he wrote his name on hers.

All in Davey's head, of course. It could have been nothing like that at all; but don't we all tell ourselves stories when we haven't got hard facts to go on? The same as looking at the future. Like his scam, Davey could see it all living and real in his head. Passing the Kentish Arms the other night, he'd seen the dog ring where he was going to padlock Claire's bike; and as he'd turned the corner into Gibraltar Road he'd seen the pub's outside gents' where he'd excuse himself to go and check the scam had worked, and the skip he'd use if it hadn't. Hard, solid *will be*; as sure in Davey's head as anything that had already gone off.

But he kept staring at the picture; because there was something else in it. There was that hope. Photos always have hope; people shine their brightest eyes for cameras, put on those *here I am* looks which don't allow for any bad luck. He looked at all those bright hopeful faces on the blokes with his grandad; how many "gonna be" lottery winners shining out there? Going by their eyes, the lot of them! And Sam and Louise; they had to have had some good years before she died . . .

But a quick frown – on account of what that old shopkeeper had said about his nan; on account of what Uncle Cyril had said about his grandad.

And how had Louise died? He had the sudden cold thought that there could be a link between her mystery death and the log book this photo had been tucked into. Had Sam crashed the car with Louise in it? Was that how she'd gone, what no one wanted to talk about?

But Davey smoothed the wrinkles off, shook off the chill. It all still bugged him to the soul, but he wasn't going to let it bug him today. Today, he'd got other fish to fry.

He put the photo in his wallet, next to his heart for luck.

And he made a start on the scam, which needed all the luck in the world ... Starting with a secret goodbye to the Wingrave, out in the garage where he wouldn't be seen by nosy neighbours.

"To his horse, to his horse
He was saying goodbye to his horse;
And as he was saying goodbye to his horse,
He was saying goodbye to his horse."

It was a daft song, sung by Davey's grandad peeling spuds or shaking out one of his endless tins of thick soup. Daft, and *sad*, because it was someone saying goodbye to a trusty steed – and wasn't the Wingrave supposed to have been that to Davey? Patting the saddle and stroking the hand-built frame, his eyes filled up and his throat hurt, remembering how many millions of miles over the moon he'd been when he'd first ridden the bike home from Carl Bell's. And his mouth filled with the boiling spit of anger at how helpless he was now, the hang-up of what he was into doing today.

Davey was going to go to the Kentish Arms, just drop in, someone in the family, passing on a run. But he was going to leave the Wingrave outside without locking it, put it in a tempting place where it couldn't NOT be nicked, not with all the dodgy youth around on half term. And after giving time for it to go, he was going to say goodbye, head off with Claire – but run back in to tell Uncle Cyril the bad news – who'd have to report the bike missing to the police: and that night his dad claimed on the insurance.

Because, being the man he was, John Booth had got the bike insured.

Getting his Wingrave nicked to get out of showing Jarvis respect, getting *rid* – because having it was too much grief.

But easy! The beauty of it being, it gave Stuart Jarvis an out. With the bike stolen for real he

154

couldn't make Davey sell it to him, could he? So he didn't lose face, and Davey bought a track bike with the insurance pay-out, something Jarvis wouldn't want.

The old red eyes – and here he was, supposed to be out with Claire for a gorgeous day! So why not go for the twist and shout of that? he asked himself – and let the nicking happen tomorrow? What a day it could be; she could kiss his tears away, in advance . . .

But Davey Booth was a Stan Barrett rider. He was fast and he was strong, and he was into tactics, he always followed Barrett's instructions to the letter. He was master at how to let go the lead, ride up the bank, tailgate the pack; and he knew when to come down off the stayers' line and go for the front – all training which put the block on him giving up. A real temptation, Claire to himself again, shoving Jarvis back under for now; but he wouldn't get free of the crook by giving in to it. No way was Jarvis going away: plus, he needed Claire at Uncle Cyril's to give it the cred it needed: a solid, cracking witness. And the plan was going to work – wouldn't Grandad have gone for it? "Proud of you, mate!" So many times, when they'd been hatching something up, the two chaps – how to get Davey an extra stay or a late pass – there'd been this strong feeling of how great the two of them would have been at dreaming up thrillers or De Niro films. There was always that exciting *operator's* edge with Grandad.

And *wasn't* there just a chance today could be saved? After the Wingrave had gone, couldn't they leave Claire's bike at Uncle Cyril's pub and go off on a bus somewhere? They could, if he took enough dosh.

With his mum and dad at work, Davey wheeled out his bike and did the security, the half-term drill: house alarm on and doors double locked. The other security he'd already taken care of; the other bit of his cover; he'd told his mum the night before that he was going out with Claire, going past Uncle Cyril's, told her he'd tell him that all the bungalow business was sorted. She'd said, "He knows it is," but, no problem – Davey had sown the seed. *Dig your groove, make your move!* Grandad would say.

Outside, he sniffed at the weather; not as nice as the Eynsford day; colder, dry but with plenty of cloud, good cycle-racing stuff. And it hit him then that he could have spent the night stewing about rain. Wouldn't a pelting with what Grandad called the wet stuff have clobbered his plans? *Blow out!* But because a rainy day wasn't how Davey had seen it, somehow that wasn't how it turned out.

But wet out or dry, Claire had dressed for the Whitsun chill. No cut-off vest and bare belly, but a hooded tracksuit top; and no long brown legs but baggy matching bottoms. Not that Davey could have noticed anything today but her eyes, her mouth, her hair.

Her hair? Before Claire, Davey had never noticed anyone's hair. But Claire's hair was different. Claire made your mouth drop open with what she did to it. Today it was all Flintstone, up like an onion, one ribbon instead of two, should have looked a sight but had him nodding at it, a dippy smile.

She'd come to the gate as he cycled up, and he'd hardly lifted his leg over the saddle.

"Do you run *on* rails, Davey Booth?"

"Eh?"

"We could set our video by you." She lifted his wrist and showed him his watch; not knowing he'd just sat round the corner for eight minutes.

And he couldn't help saying it. "Great hair!"

"*Ten* points."

"Uh?"

"For noticing." And she kissed him on the nose.

On the nose? Less than lips, more than the cheek; jokey but a very *private* kiss, on the nose.

Very special. Davey reckoned Nigel Kennedy didn't get any of those – a "hello" worlds different to her "goodbye" the other Saturday.

He had to have a glass brain, because she saw right into it. "My dad was watching last time. Conserving *in* the conservatory."

"You mean *ob*serving."

"I mean *con*serving. Conserving my purity." And she showed him the tip of her tongue. Just the pink tip.

Which all but did for Davey. Scam? Scram! For want of saying it, he'd blow out the Kentish Arms and head straight for the Sevenoaks road.

But Claire said something first. "He's expecting us."

"Your dad?"

"My grandad. 'Uncle Cyril'. Mum told him we're calling in, though she *didn't* know why."

"Good ol' Mum!" Rot her!

So the course was set, the great downhill, from the posh roads of Bromley to the ragged streets round the Kentish Arms. And taking them very little time at all.

Where, in his own kingdom, Uncle Cyril was definitely the guv'nor. Shining-shaved, tall, loud voice, white shirt dazzling among the singlets and slogans of the drinkers in the bar. He smiled his tile-white teeth and came round from behind the taps, leaving the serving to a woman called Pam; his long, circling arms protecting his grand-daughter from the Kentish Arms roughs.

He nodded to Davey. "Boy."

Davey's belly boiled. Why did all the cantan-kerous old buffers like Uncle Cyril go on for ever when the good old good 'uns like Grandad popped off so young? But Davey gave him a quick smile like a proper visitor and followed him under an arch into an alcove with a settle, two chairs and a pay phone.

"You've come to a rough ol' neck of the woods on your tod," the old man's teeth clicked at Claire.

"*That's* because I've come with him." She gave Davey a beamer of a smile that filled the gloomy room with gold. "*Bit* of business."

But Davey knew he'd already done the business; he'd chained up Claire's bike, sent her on ahead to the pub door while he fiddled with his own – and left it well clear of the lock; a gift from heaven! Just two more tickles now. Give Uncle Cyril the "message" from his mum, and get to the outside lav to chuck the Wingrave in the skip if it hadn't been nicked.

Uncle Cyril didn't ask them what they wanted to drink. Pam was bringing a bent old tray with two Cokes and a couple of packets of crisps; all the usual handing round, taking and thanking, while Davey wound himself up for what he was going to say. His reason for coming ...

Uncle Cyril folded his arms, sitting facing Davey and Claire as if he were still standing up. No pipe, no crossed legs, no real time for a social call before his big screen coloured up with racing from Doncaster.

"So, what's this all about?"

And even as he said it – the best he could do – Davey's message sounded tinpot. "Right. Well, it's just ... Mum says, she wants you to know ..."

"Yeah? Gawd, spit it out, boy."

"Well, just, everything went all right with the bungalow, our end. The clearance, and the council. No problem, she said ..."

"That it?"

"What she said ..."

"Didn't reckon there *would* be any problem. It was all done tidy." But Uncle Cyril was saying it to Claire, like some big mystery – who *is* this nutty boy? *What stupid oick of a cousin have you dragged out here?* "Nice of your mum," he said, but jerking his head at the pay phone. "Ain't she never heard of one o' them?" And his laugh was like the kill of a machine gun.

Claire seemed to have got a broom handle stuck down her tracksuit, she was sitting up so straight.

"*Mug! One o' Simple Simon's firm!*" was what Grandad would have called him. Not thought out A1 at all. Davey's head had been so filled up with Jarvis and the unloading of the Wingrave, so almighty chuffed had he been with his Kentish Arms insurance scam that he hadn't done any decent homework. It was as if what he was handing in was getting slung back at him NWM – not worth marking.

And the way Claire and Uncle Cyril were looking at him, the silence in the alcove against the Jurassic Park gambling box pinging and bleeping and coughing coins, something very special by way of getting up out of the saddle was called for. Davey had to pull *something* out to keep himself in the going.

"My grandad," he suddenly said.

Uncle Cyril looked at him with the blank face of a blind man.

"You said something at the funeral . . ."

Claire rode up on her broomstick. "*Oh*, no!" She put a hand on her hip, the old *I don't believe this!*

"Be the day, boy, when I don't say something.

161

Be the day when they shove me through the curtains myself, that will ..."

"You said you hoped the old devil rotted in hell ..." It was out. On a great rush of adrenalin, Davey had said it. Claire had turned her back on him, but Davey was locked on, eye to eye with Uncle Cyril.

Who swallowed his great Adam's apple ready for saying something so serious it took a lean forward and a grip of his old knees with two leopard spot hands.

"Some sort of new boy 'ere, Cyril ...?" A walking tattoo in a vest had just come in. "You got a bike, son?"

Davey just about nodded.

"You nearly didn't 'ave! You don' leave nothin' without Fort Knox round it down these streets ..."

"I thought I had ..."

"Nah. I've brung it in for you."

"What about the other one?" Claire wanted to know.

"Done up tight all right. But you nearly lost a good bike, son."

If the man expected a drink on the guv'nor he was disappointed. Uncle Cyril hadn't taken his eyes off Davey through all this.

"It's in the bar. The bike."

"Cheers!" *Thanks a bunch!* The stupid, interfering straight goer! Why couldn't he have had off with it himself?

But Uncle Cyril was still roasting Davey with his old eyes. "You reckon I'm supposed to have said that?"

With Claire still on her feet. "It's *nothing*, Grandad. He's just—"

But even she wasn't going to stop the rush of this pack.

"You said it in the funeral car."

"*Did* I?" He hadn't moved, was still leaning forward at Davey, his breath rattling in his pipes.

Claire cleared her throat with the same odd emphasis as the way she spoke. But it was a getting-off-the-track sound – leave me out of this.

"An' they say you shouldn't speak ill of the dead . . ." Uncle Cyril said it humbly, like a gentle rap of his own knuckles.

"You wished him *worse* than dead."

The old man was shaking his head, he was closing his eyes as if there were a chance Davey might be away on the bike when he opened them.

"I spoke out of turn, boy."

"You still spoke." Because, *why* let him off? For Davey right now everything had fouled up. The bike hadn't been nicked. Jarvis was still breathing hard and stinking down his neck. Claire was wearing that same face as the night in Grandad's shed. So why shouldn't Davey push Uncle Cyril? What else had he got to lose by finding out about his grandad? At least he'd have had one result out of this grotty day.

"Stupid old man, I am. Your mothers won't forgive me. He *was* their father."

"Why won't they forgive you? Don't they know what you meant?"

"Oh, they know all right. But they won't want you to know..."

Right now the telephone alcove was like a cell with no door. No way out.

"Oh, for *good*ness' sake, Grandad. I'm old enough to have babies! I'm old enough to know. If it's a family secret, *I'm* family, aren't I? So's he." Meaning Davey, but only with a flip of the hand.

Davey looked at her, looked at Uncle Cyril; suddenly felt scared, because Grandad hadn't meant anything to anyone as much as he'd meant to Davey Booth.

And now he didn't *want* to know.

"Come on, let's get on our bikes. If it's a secret like that, I'm off out of it." He got up.

But no way was Claire coming. "You can *get* on your bike! It's the end of the ride for me." She turned back to her other grandfather, the one still living and breathing. "He's got me over here *for* this. Now he's bottling it. But I'm *not* budging till you tell me. I'll go home and say you said *all sorts* if you don't tell me what I'm entitled to know..."

"Oh." Uncle Cyril ached himself on to his feet. "A bit o' blackmail!" His teeth rattled in his mouth as he walked through to the bar. "Then I need a cup o' tea. Come one, wi' me – upstairs."

"*And* ...?"

"And I'll tell you. For my sins."

Tight, blank-faced, the short procession went, under the flap of the bar and up the private stairs, no one's eyes meeting anyone else's.

To be taken into the family sanctum where the truth could be told about Sam Butler.

Chapter Thirteen

"HE WAS a villain. A Category 'A' crook. A real no-gooder, an' he *done* for the family, total, cooked every blessed goose going . . ."

Uncle Cyril had sat them up at the dining table as if this were the School Council: him in the chair, Davey and Claire on either side, one big cup of tea, two bottles of Coke and two glasses.

But there wouldn't be any taking of notes. Not a word he was saying was ever going to be forgotten; certainly not by Davey Booth – not about his grandad.

"You mean he was a bit 'fly', a wheeler-dealer, a—"

"I mean he was a *villain*, an out an' out bad 'un. A right handful, 'tasty' – a real hard man. He'd break your arm soon as look at you . . ."

Davey gripped his Coke, wanted to sling it in Uncle Cyril's long, toothy face, glass and all – the rotten, jealous *liar*. Just because he was a sad old man and Grandad had been the great bloke he was . . .

"No good looking at me that way, boy. It's God's truth I'm telling you. I should know, his blessed cousin, born in the next road over Camberwell . . ."

But Davey just shook his head, wanted to stuff his fingers in his ears.

"Started small, o' course, little tea-leaf – baggage handler over Heathrow; started taking note of the addresses off a few holiday labels, then paid the empty drums a visit – that sort of touch . . . But 'e soon fell foul of the big boys, Tony Lewis . . ."

Davey had heard of Tony Lewis; they wrote real-life gangster paperbacks about him. But there was no believing all this rubbish.

"Lewis's firm was just gettin' south o' the river all sewn up. This was their patch, so Sam Butler has to take a pasting for bein' so cheeky, then he either beats 'em or he joins 'em." Uncle Cyril took a sucking at his tea. "But there *wasn't* no beating 'em, not till the law done it over a shooting – so 'e joined 'em. A strong arm, a straightener, a frightener. That's what your grandad was."

"No!" Davey pushed at the table. The old beggar was making this up. Davey's grandad had been kind, funny, *loving*. He was one of the two chaps. He'd never once so much as shouted at Davey, he wasn't any villainous hard man.

"Sit down, boy, mind that drink!"

Davey sat and folded his arms, tight.

"See, Lewis was gettin' on to all the rackets; had the dog-racing in his pocket, ran some girls, took protection money off the little spielers where the gambling went on. Like, you pay Tony Lewis, an' no one breaks up your joint. That's 'ow it worked ..."

Davey stared. *Spieler.* That was a word he'd heard before. When he and Grandad had been at it at cards, and Davey had wanted a few pence on the result. *What d'you think I am 'ere, a spieler?* But then tons of people knew all sorts of words ...

"What Butler went down for in the end was doing over a gang who never got the message. They went in firm-handed an' smashed up a Lewis bookies', so Butler taught 'em to respect 'ow things was run ..."

"*By* doing what?" asked Claire.

Which already Davey didn't want to hear.

"By *enlarging* one kid with a white hot poker, an' breaking his mates' arms between two bricks." Uncle Cyril mimed the chop, and Claire closed her eyes. Davey wanted to close his, but he couldn't so much as blink; he had to keep on staring at Uncle Cyril who was talking to him, straight.

"Ruined your nan, Sam Butler did. Had her doing his threatening for him. She took herself off young, died of a mix o' shame and overcooked loyalty, did Louise. An' he had me running this place like his private meet. Wanna do a deal, pay your respects? See you in the Kentish. We never 'ad lives to call our own, none of us . . ."

Like ripping his eyes away from a snake, Davey got a quick look at Claire. She was stirring her drink with a finger and sucking it; no eyes for anyone, nor ears. Davey swallowed, not on Coke, but on a gob of his pride. Because wasn't this talk about his nan something the same as the old woman in the shop had been saying? *Was* there some twist of the truth in some of this? *Did* some of this hold up?

It did if you believed in fairy stories! Strewth, for God's *sake*! "No!" he shouted down the table. "Mum told me about him – he worked his guts out all over, earning a living, sending money back home . . ."

"All over?" Another slurp of tea. "All over where?"

"Australia . . ."

"*Australia?!* No, boy. Parkhurst, Wanno, the

169

Scrubs. Category 'A' banged up, that's where he was."

"Prison?"

"Done *years* inside, Sam Butler. He stank of prison. Everything he said stank of prison. Can't you hear it? 'Diesel' for his tea, 'hotplate' for his oven, 'reader' for his book. All stir lingo. An' his prison ways – mashing up his grub so the naff stuff didn't taste, endless tins of soup 'cos no one can get at your soup, his 'snout' for smoking – it come off him like a reek, prison did. I tell you, he saw more of inside than he ever saw of 'all over'."

Davey downed the last of his Coke, didn't know how he swallowed it, but did it for something to do. He had to think, because in spite of himself, some of this was holding up.

"Was he a murderer, then?" Claire wanted to know, but making herself sound bored, asking. "Did he kill anyone?"

Uncle Cyril shook his head, looking almost reluctant not to be able to nod. "He stopped short of that, I'll give you – but more b' luck than judgement. Armed robbery, he went all tooled up for that – *an'* the cutlery he carried other times. Sword. Machetty. Took a razor to the pictures. Swung a bike chain like nobody's business. See, when Tony Lewis *wanted* someone straightened, it was Sam Butler he sent round to do it."

Davey breathed in deep, blew it out. Against everything he *wanted* to think about his grandad he was having to start believing this hateful old man: that those hands which had tightened the spokes on his bike, the grip he'd used to shift a stubborn nut, those fingers that had gently dabbed oil on a gear cable – all the skilled and helpful things they'd done – they'd all once been used to dish out pain and punishment. And hadn't he always liked schemes and scams, had that operator's edge?

"But when he come out the last time, end of his twelve, Tony Lewis was gone, the world had moved on, an' Butler had had the fires damped down inside. He come out *old*, a tiger without no teeth, who crawled around, made promises to your mums, an' found himself a bush to lie under, and die."

But only after those great years of being Davey's grandad! "He had teeth to me!" Davey shouted.

Uncle Cyril ignored it. "He'd gone soft. Come out on licence, kep' his nose clean had to report to the probation once a week an' get his book signed . . ."

Davey was numb. His skin was cold, his inside ice, his brain in a coma. Everything, everything,

everything he'd believed about his grandad had been a great lie. There in the upstairs of the Kentish Arms, it was like being told there wasn't any God. The most destructive thing that could happen to Davey was the being told all this about a man he'd loved to death. And it was too much, too much to take in, too much to even *start* reckoning. Well, how could he ever get his head round something like this?

The tea cup chinked on Uncle Cyril's teeth, and just to show that he could still move a muscle, Davey pulled out his wallet, and the picture from Margate. By way of trying to find words, he looked at it, and Uncle Cyril reached over and took it.

"I remember this. They're all here," the old man said. He rubbed a finger along the line of blokes. "Lewis's lot, knew 'em all. After Butler came on the scene they used this pub like their front office." A horny old nail scratched at face after face. "Died on the Island; ran off to Tossa; still on the blag; topped by the Bradshaws the other side of the water... They was doing a bit o' business this day, sorting the Margate boys ..."

"And Nan, Louise ... That's her there?" Davey got out.

"And Louise," he nodded, "and me ..."

"*You?*" Claire's head was suddenly up again; and she took the photo.

"Well, who drove their Roller? Who *had* to go, under the thumb?"

But Davey didn't care which one of them was Uncle Cyril.

"All tarred with his brush, we was. Her. Louise. She ended up pretending she liked the life, ran the roost round these streets till she fell for the twins – your mums; till she couldn't split herself in two no more an' ran her car off Beachy Head . . ."

"Eh?!"

"Vauxhall Victor. Her in it. What you've got to see is, bullies like Sam Butler 'ave to have the power, they *live off* the respect. When she couldn't bear to pay him no more o' that, she done the other thing."

"She *killed* herself?"

"Accidental, of course – they said. But then he had the doctor in his pocket, didn't he? It was the Council brought your mums up."

Davey thought he was going to be sick, all over the oak: at the strength of things about his grandad, at what his nan had done. There wasn't any room for ifs or buts any more. What he was staring in the face was the fact that his grandad had been a bully of the worst sort going. No wonder his mum had kept the man at arm's length; no wonder his dad was never happy about his boy being round there so much ...

And who did Sam Butler put Davey in mind of?

Stuart Jarvis. The man he'd known as Grandad didn't exist any more. There was just this picture of a tasty Stuart Jarvis.

Davey got up, looked at Claire, stood with the twist of going.

"You *get* off, then," she said.

He shrugged. "Not coming?" Why ask?

"*No* way! You've had your day made, Davey Booth, if *not* the way you planned it. Thanks *a* million!" And she refilled her glass from her Coke bottle. "You're *just* lucky I can't be arsed to get up and smack your selfish face!"

"Claire ..."

"Don't *Claire* me!" Her face had turned ugly with hate. Even the gorgeous Claire's.

So Davey left the photo where it was, on the table, didn't say a thank you, pushed out of the room, down the stairs and under the flap to lay hand on his Wingrave.

Which was still there. The bike he hadn't reckoned on riding home.

*

He still rode well; he still swerved round the rough bumps, squeezed at his brakes when tail lights lit; flicked down gears when the traffic walked. He could have given up, come off, gone under a bus after what he'd just taken in the face, that stuff he'd had slung at him from all directions; but a good rider's always a good rider – even with the different hurts getting at him in so many different places. The frozen sweat, the eggshell of ice all over him at the drop-dead news that his grandad had been a crook. The choke in his throat at the jealousy of not being the same Davey Booth he'd been with Claire the last time. And the adrenalin grip in his middle that here he was still riding the Wingrave. In every direction he looked there was grief – the oily back of this bus, the heavy threat of that lorry, the killer exhaust of that van – everything in Davey's life that could have been good was rotten.

Everything. And on top of the rest, by racing off with Claire at Crystal Palace he'd blown himself out of the London Youth Games. Worse, Claire thought he'd only pretended to like her so he could get at Uncle Cyril.

Davey saw a gap in the traffic and went for it. For fifty metres he put his head down as if he might leave everything behind, burn it all off. But, like the heavy lorry, it caught up with him again at the lights.

And thudding in his head, rolling in his stomach, was the terrible truth of it. Grandad was a Jarvis. Sam Butler had done to his victims what Jarvis did in the school lavs and down dark alleys; he was Jarvis in the adult version. Davey could even hear in his head the way the old man would have said things. *Got the dosh, Solly, 'cos if you ain't you're gonna get cut!* And down from his sleeve would drop a knife as wide as a hand. Or, *Can't take no more o' your lip, son, you're gonna get taught a bit of respect* ... And in with the hammer, or the chain, or the knuckleduster, whichever tool was favourite for the job. Expert. Hard. No sympathy or second chances. Just needing that respect. Like Jarvis.

Davey's cracking pace kept up with the racing of his mind; in and out of vehicles, taking chances with a brake or a down-gear spurt. He'd read about their crooked sort, the London mob, seen them in films – all prison lean, with hard eyes and big dangling hands; smashing up lives everywhere on no more than a fancy. And all the talking they did, their words and what they went on about, wasn't that how his grandad had sounded when you really listened to it?

The firm, the chaps – that had to be crook and prison talk. And his ways, like Uncle Cyril said – his love of that yard of sky in his garden, the luxury of a draughts board with all the pieces; how he stared at people and they backed off from arguing. *And didn't Davey know there'd have been no Jarvis problem if his grandad had been up and about?*

So had he sussed it somehow? Had Davey always felt a dangerous edge to the man?

He cracked on, kept well clear of Claire's Bromley, rode through Catford, came over Shooters Hill and pedalled fast in high gear down to the lights at the common, his head up into the racing breeze as if it might blow everything through and out of him.

Crook.

Villain.

Straightener.

Heavy.

Hit man.

Face.

That's what his grandad was, all that, the man he'd loved as a kind and gentle pensioner, his special mate – a spiteful south London crook to whom everyone had to show respect.

And, sure! *Just* like Jarvis – who didn't live two

minutes from here in this same part of the world. Because, which way had Davey come? In the same way as he'd somehow given the miss to Bromley, Davey was cycling *this* way back home, the long way round, through Jarvis territory. Accidentally or on purpose.

And with a flap of his hand, he was leaning over into Jarvis's turning.

Accidentally? Purposely? *Madly!* What the hell was he up to? he asked himself. What stroke was this he was pulling?

Like watching someone else doing it, Davey was getting off his bike and knocking on Jarvis's door. Sort of, *Can Stuart come out to play, Mrs Jarvis?*

Not!

The door opened, crashed against the passage wall as loud as it slamming shut.

"Boove!" Jarvis was sorting his trousers. "Well, good boy, son!"

Davey couldn't lay hold on words. With all the talking in his head, he was out of words for real. He took off his lid.

"I ain't got the dosh like *that*!"

Davey found some words. "Don't matter."

"Magic!" Jarvis was less blowy on his own doormat, but he still had those slits of eyes needling out that he was top man.

"Come over the common, Jarvis."

"Anywhere, son." He was wiping his mouth, shoving a mat in the door. "Try it anywhere."

"Over the common, then." And Davey walked away.

Chapter Fourteen

DAVEY DIDN'T wait for him, he wasn't letting Jarvis ride the Wingrave to the common. He got on the bike and cycled out of the turning, across the main road and over to where there was a flat arena of thick, long grass, the sort that looks like getting on for being wheat.

Jarvis came walking behind, swaggering, all shoulder and kick; crossed the road to the grass with a hand at someone's windscreen.

Who didn't hoot.

Davey saw him coming through the gorse, out of sight of the traffic now, the Wingrave lying in the long grass.

"What's this? On the road, son! I *got* a mountin' bike ..."

"Yeah, but you haven't got a hand-built Wingrave. Not yet." Davey stood and stared him in the muggy face. "Only, 'f you want this one, Jarvis, you gotta *kill* me for it, right? 'Cos it ain't for sale ..."

"Do what?" Jarvis's face had suddenly set in the cast of a Roman statue; the stony snarl of the pro gladiator.

"You heard. Come on, *Stuart*, if you think you're hard enough, do what you've been mouthing about . . ."

Jarvis sneered. "If I touch you, Boove, you're dead, you know that?"

"Dead, or up A and E – you'll still be watching the Wingrave rust from behind whatever bars they shove toe-rags like you . . ."

"Yeah?" Jarvis was taking in a tyreful of air, bunching his hands, holding himself primed. "Two kids c'n 'ave a fight, Boove. You c'n say it's the bike, I c'n say you slagged off my ol' mum, so I learned you a bit o' respect . . ."

True. And Davey had never been so scared in his life. He was in for a bloody fight royale, a killer. Bluff hadn't worked, as if he'd ever thought it would, which left him thirty seconds off being beaten to the look of a car-flattened cat – a countdown which made his scare come out on no more than a high tremble. He had to keep coughing to get at the words.

"But, whatever . . . you can . . . tell your little mates . . . I never sold you . . . the bike." Davey stood with his own arms hanging. "You want . . .

181

respect? I've got more o' that . . . for cack down the pan!" He was hyping himself, breathing deep, pre-race stuff. And the words were coming easier, because insults did. "You need hell knocking out of you, Dog's-breath!"

And Davey ran at him; saw that quick look of Jarvis startle as to what stunt he was pulling. Some wimp not *fighting* him, was he? But there wasn't any stunt. Just a fist, which Davey flailed at Jarvis's head like a balloon on concrete.

Jarvis didn't mess about, didn't dance around. His two meaty hands grabbed hold of Davey's shoulders and pulled him fierce on to a head butt. Crack! Not full on to break his nose – Davey was still twisted after his punch – but crunch on to the glance of his cheek. Bone on bone, an eye closer, but more shock than real hurt. Leaving Davey at the back of his balance with Jarvis coming in again, left fist, right fist – stone hard punches that thudded into a shoulder, clattered the other cheek, swung Davey's head into a flattened profile, his nose going round to meet his ear.

Which should have been enough to have Davey down, for the kicking. But somehow he kept his feet. Punches came in, a heart stopper to the chest, a gut tearer in the belly, another rock to the head which almost twisted it off his neck – picked, vicious, damaging punches – but Davey somehow keeping from falling over and even getting one or two in himself. Jarvis not defending – he'd never have to defend after what he'd dished out – so Davey's punches found their own light mark. Mosquito stings, flea bites on a rhino; but not done for the landing but for the *punching*. Davey taking it, taking it, taking it – blood, snot, chipped teeth, cracked ribs, only one eye to see through: but none of it stopping him while he could swing, punch, kick and tear at Jarvis. Doing *some* damage, landing a lucky one on Jarvis's nose that would bung him up for a bit. Snorting, blind, angry, tenacious, a fight Davey could never win but a fight he was ready to die in; a fight to the death because he wasn't fighting Jarvis, he hadn't been from the start; he hadn't been up against Jarvis from the moment he'd gone Jarvis's way home.

He was fighting the first Sam Butler. Whatever it cost him, he was punching, kicking, tearing, hammering, *knocking the devil out of his grandad.*

Thud! Crack! Against a thug who wouldn't know when to stop, no more than Davey would. A lung splitter to Davey's chest that seemed to kill his heart, but a run forward on the last gasp and a blind, lucky butt that got Jarvis in the belly, and took him off his balance.

Over backwards, and Davey still going forwards for another flap to Jarvis's face with just enough force to tip him. Over into the long grass, and crack on to the hand-built frame of the Wingrave, a toe grip up into the tail of Jarvis's spine.

"Faaoouw!"

And Jarvis was lying there, eyes wide, mouth gawping, shaking small but paralysed big – Davey standing sucking in air, snivelling, dribbling, bleeding, breathing hot and hard and rattly; tottering, forcing himself to stay alive and on his feet like a dog come out of a car crash.

Jarvis lifted a hand to him. A hand which was shaking for help, his eyes blinking the words because the mouth was locked mute open.

But Davey found some. "You ... wanted ... on to the Wingrave. You're on it now, son!"

He should have crawled somewhere for help; he shouldn't have tried to help Jarvis, not if he had spinal damage, splayed there on the hand-built. But this was *private*, this was Davey standing and the dead devil in his grandad lying there. What he was doing was for Sam Butler. Even if it did for Jarvis, Davey was going to pull him up.

He came round behind, the wet of the fight dripping all over, and with the last of his strength he heaved Jarvis to his feet, like someone righting a statue after a war.

And Jarvis stood, and balanced, and somehow stayed.

Davey came round in front of him, one eye swollen tight shut, and helped him totter forward from the Wingrave to find the life in his legs.

"You c'n walk," mumbled Davey through blood and spit, "and I can talk. But don't you ever come at me again, right? You want the bike, you take it now . . ."

Jarvis stared at Davey, rubbed a hand down at the base of his being. "Stuff the bike, Boove, an' stuff you!" He started shuffling towards the edge of the common. "But this is just you an' me, right?"

"You an' me. Else I'm dead meat. You said, before." And, feeling like dead meat right now, Davey hoiked his bike up off the grass and hobbled towards home, leaning heavy on its hand-built frame, but feeling lighter in his complicated heart.

He knew what had happened – he'd spiked Jarvis by a lucky push; but lucky pushes don't happen if you haven't been pushing in the first place. And Davey had been driven hard to do what he'd done. Luck never comes your way unless you're up for it; you don't win the Wincanton/Leeds without you enter for it. By being driven, he'd beaten Jarvis as real as if he'd been a better fighter; because what was real in life was what happened. Not myth. Not history. Davey had knocked devils out of what Jarvis had stood for; out of what Sam Butler had been; and that was as real as the blood on Davey's shirt.

And as he pushed the Wingrave home, the long way, past his grandad's bungalow where there were new curtains up, Davey knew that nothing in the world could take away what had been real about his grandad, to him.

A loving grandad. A great "oppo". Still one of the two chaps who used to eat and drink and talk and play games in there. For Davey, there would never ever be any other Grandad so real.

Davey's dad bounced his shock and rage off all four walls. He couldn't believe what he saw! Davey's mum shrieked, hugged her boy, was halfway to the hospital with him. But Davey wasn't having it.

No – it was nothing to do with Claire – it was some grief he'd had, and he'd sorted it. He shouted at them, cried, refused the police, refused the doctor, *he was all right!* He'd fought one of his own battles – and he'd won it. And he even managed to clench a fist in victory.

"Is this any stick from your rotten grandad . . .?"

Davey even got his swollen eye open to give the glare to his father. "He was never rotten to me!"

But he had to give in to Dettol and Savlon, backing off all the while, up on his toes to get away.

And as soon as he could, watched by two pairs of eyes staring more at each other than at him, he went to his room and found a pen and some paper.

Where he did his best to write a letter to Claire, to explain himself, to lay himself open, to tell her everything for real, *his* real – missing nothing out, with nothing smudged or nearly true; telling her he hoped like hell she could forgive him.

Because he loved her. That was for real, too. And he *was* going to use that word. If you're old enough to hate, you're old enough to love.

But he had to give up; his hand was too swollen and shaky. With the fight still coming off him, the only way he could grip the pen was like a dagger, and the marks he was making were like violence on paper.

So he went back downstairs, and out to the hand-built Wingrave, which he somehow managed to ride – and headed off for Bromley, with no looking over his shoulder any more. To Claire's, where he was going to say it all instead.

And never mind the state he was in. If she heard him out, and she felt like it, she could *just* find room to kiss him again on the nose.

ORCHARD BLACK APPLES

Freedom Flight	Bernard Ashley	1 84121 306 3	£4.99
Little Soldier	Bernard Ashley	1 86039 879 0	£4.99
Revenge House	Bernard Ashley	1 84121 814 6	£4.99
Going Straight	Michael Coleman	1 84362 299 8	£4.99
Tag	Michael Coleman	1 84362 182 7	£4.99
Weirdo's War	Michael Coleman	1 84362 183 5	£4.99
Horowitz Horror	Anthony Horowitz	1 84121 455 8	£4.99
More Horowitz Horror	Anthony Horowitz	1 84121 607 0	£4.99
Get a Life	Jean Ure	1 84121 831 6	£4.99